SECRETS OF WILDFLOWER ISLAND

WILDFLOWER MYSTERY SERIES - BOOK 1

MICHELLE FILES

Edited by
CECILY BROOKES

BOOKLOVERS PUBLISHING

INTRODUCTION

When four teenage girls discover a body, badly beaten, a nice day at the beach goes horribly wrong.

As they embark on a quest to solve the murder, they find themselves as the main suspects. The girls quickly turn on each other as they are blackmailed by an unknown person and harassed by others.

Who killed the boy? Will the girls be next?

This mesmerizing mystery, suspense novel will have you guessing until the end.

Book 1 in the Wildflower Mystery Series.

Novels by Michelle Files:

TYLER MYSTERY SERIES:
Girl Lost
A Reckless Life

WILDFLOWER MYSTERY SERIES:
Secrets of Wildflower Island
Desperation on Wildflower Island
Storm on Wildflower Island
Thorns on Wildflower Island

IVY WELLS MYSTERY SERIES:
The Many Lives of Ivy Wells
The Many Lives of Sam Wells
The Many Lives of Jack Wells

STONE MOUNTAIN FAMILY SAGA:
Winters Legend on Stone Mountain
A Dangerous Game on Stone Mountain
Deceit on Stone Mountain

For information on any of Michelle's books:
www.MichelleFiles.com

Copyright © 2017 by Michelle Files
All rights reserved. No part of this publication may be reproduced, distributed, or transmitted in any form, without prior written permission of the author.

Published in the United States by BookLovers Publishing.
Edited by Cecily Brookes and BookLovers Publishing.

This is a work of fiction. Any similarities to actual people, places or events is purely coincidental.

2nd Edition 2020

CHAPTER 1

The shaking earth stopped the beach party preparations. Tim reached over the table to steady the drinks from spilling over.

A rumbling began creeping toward the shore. Some noticed. Some did not.

"Tim, are we having an earthquake?" Roxanne asked, her eyes wide.

He looked out over the ocean. He saw nothing unusual, but that didn't matter. Tim had lived on Wildflower Island his entire life. He knew what the dull roar meant. He could feel the blood draining from his face, as it turned ashen. He could feel the terror deep down into his soul.

"Roxanne run! Everybody run!" he screamed.

A few hours earlier…

"Mary, where is your sister? We have something we want to talk to you about," Tim asked his daughter as the family sat down to have a nice lunch at the Wildflower Inn Cafe they owned.

"She went to the beach party," Mary replied, propping her bare feet up on the remaining empty chair, her pink sparkly toenail polish gleaming in the sun.

"I'm here, I'm here." Piper ran up the wooden stairs from the beach onto the cafe's deck. "Can we make this quick? I want to go back down to the party. Mary, move." Piper pushed her sister's feet off of her chair. She sat down and began braiding her long blonde hair while she waited for their parents to tell them whatever it was they wanted. Getting back to having fun with her friends was the only thing on her mind that sunny summer day.

The teenaged waitress took their lunch orders immediately upon them sitting down at their usual table, which interrupted their conversation. She ignored the other customers who had arrived several minutes before and were still waiting for her to address them. Frankie was receiving irritated looks from quite a few tables, of which she was completely oblivious to. This did not go unnoticed by Tim Carmichael, Piper and Mary's father. He ran the cafe and it was important to him that his customers were well taken care of.

Frankie was just 16 years old and had a head full of wild red hair. With her curves and just a few freckles on her nose, she was very cute, and a favorite of the local boys that frequented the cafe. She didn't pay them much attention though, which drove them even crazier. She was wearing nothing but cut off jean shorts, a bikini top, and flip flops. This was the standard wear at the outdoor cafe on the beach.

Frankie smiled back at Tim and wandered off to help the rest of her customers.

Once she was out of earshot, Tim turned back to his family.

"As I was saying, we have something your mom and I want to talk to you about."

Piper and Mary were 15 years old and identical twins. So identical that even Tim and Roxanne had trouble sometimes telling their daughters apart. It was usually their personalities that were easily distinguishable, rather than their looks. They had long, wavy blonde hair and piercing powder blue eyes. They were the envy of every girl in school, and most of the local boys had a crush on one or both of them.

Piper was easily the more outgoing of the two. The social butterfly of the family, her father called her. Because of this, kids her age were naturally drawn to her. Mary was a bit more shy. Certainly not an introvert, but she did not have the fearless, outgoing personality that Piper had. When they were with a group of friends, it was always Piper holding court, while Mary stood in the background, mostly unnoticed.

"I'll tell them," Roxanne said to her husband, taking his hand. She saw the relief on his face as she steadied his trembling hands. "Your dad and I have decided to separate."

Piper stopped braiding her hair and let it unravel on its own, as her hands dropped to her lap. "What do you mean?" Piper asked. She was temporarily caught off guard.

Mary sat quietly, taking it all in. She was biting her lower lip and twisting her hair, like she did anytime she got nervous about something. She did what she usually did, she let Piper do all the talking.

"She means," Tim responded, "that I will be moving out…for now at least. We are not talking about getting divorced right now. We just want to see how it goes."

He knew how that must have sounded to the twins. 'See how it goes?' It sounded like they didn't take their marriage seriously. Not seriously enough to try their best to work it out, but that wasn't the case. They had been in marriage counseling for months and it just wasn't getting any better.

Tim knew that their troubles were mostly his fault. He liked to spend a lot of his time at the pub down the street. Though there was a bar at the inn they owned, he needed time away. Away from his wife, kids, and the constant threat of work. Because they lived at the business they owned, he could never get away from always being at work.

Anything had to be better than the constant bickering that went on between the two of them. It didn't just stay within the walls of their house either. It extended to the streets of Sea Cove.

Tim looked around to see if anyone had heard them. They knew just about everyone in town and didn't need to be the latest topic of gossip. He was almost positive that it probably didn't matter anyway.

Their fights were sometimes public. Very public. He really did love her, but Tim and Roxanne were gasoline and a lit match when they got going.

The family spent the next half hour talking about the split. The twins were understandably upset by it, but that day they were having trouble concentrating. The beach beckoned them.

It was the annual 'beginning of summer' party that the teenagers on the island threw. It was always on the first day of summer vacation and was an all day party. It lasted long into the night. Tim and Roxanne had catered the party for quite a few years, somehow becoming the unofficial chaperones.

When it appeared to the twins that the conversation was over, Piper jumped in. "Can we go now? We are missing everything!"

"Yes, fine. Go," Roxanne said, her blue eyes sparkling in the bright sunshine.

Before she finished her sentence, both girls were running for the beach. The Carmichaels couldn't help but smile at their enthusiasm.

"It's really slow here today." Tim and Roxanne turned to see Frankie standing next to their table, looking longingly at the beach, her red hair drifting about in the breeze.

"Go," Tim said, waving his hand toward the beach. "We'll clean up these dishes."

With that, Frankie kicked off her flip flops and sauntered down the steps to the beach.

CHAPTER 2

Tim and Roxanne Carmichael bought the Wildflower Inn and Cafe shortly after they married 18 years prior. It was Roxanne's job to run the inn. Tim ran the cafe and did the general handyman work. Though neither of them had ever run a company of any kind before, it didn't take long for Roxanne to become a shrewd business woman. She worked hard and was really good at her job. Even though they bought a rundown, poorly managed inn and cafe, as soon as they remodeled and started advertising, they were making a profit. The cafe, with its fresh seafood specials was a favorite of the locals and tourists alike.

Wildflower Island, or 'The Island,' as the locals called it, was a huge tourist destination. Off the coast of California, it was a favorite vacation spot with its warm, sunny weather most days of the year. Therefore, Sea Cove was busy all year. However, summer was still their busiest time. Because there are a few ski resorts in California, many people go on ski vacations during the winter, to places like Big Bear and Wrightwood. Summer was reserved for Wildflower Island. There were a couple of other small towns on the other side of the hills, but the town of Sea Cove was where everyone vacationed.

"Do you know where Anna is?" Roxanne asked her husband as they remained seated, watching the teens on the beach.

"No. Haven't seen her." I just assumed that she was down there." He pointed toward the ever increasing sea of teenagers.

"I'm going to go look for her." Roxanne stood up. "That girl spends way too much time in the office. She needs to get out and have fun for a change."

It did help the bottom line of the Wildflower Inn that some of their employees were barely paid troubled teenage girls, such as Anna and Frankie. The town affectionately called them 'The Wildflowers.' The girls had gotten into some trouble and most had been arrested, though not all of them. The Wildflower Inn acted as a type of halfway house for the girls. Some were put there by the state, and the Carmichaels were paid to house and feed them. Other girls just showed up on their doorstep, looking for help. The teens lived and worked there in exchange for free room and board, and a small salary. That was how Roxanne got the inn out of the red, with cheap labor.

Over the years, the teens came and went. Some went back home, some had moved on, and some ended up in jail. The Carmichaels were proud of the fact that roughly 80% of 'their girls' went on to become productive human beings, with just an occasional one going to jail. Those were always girls that came to them very troubled and they just couldn't reach them, no matter how hard they tried.

At the moment, there were only two wayward teens living at the Wildflower: Frankie and Anna. Frankie was 16 years old and moved in with them just two months earlier. She was not a trouble maker at all. Her mother's boyfriend was a mean drunk. Frankie begged her mother to leave, but she wouldn't. That's when Frankie decided that she would not live her life with that man, any man actually, beating her down. Her mother had a string of loser boyfriends. Frankie had enough.

One day, Frankie walked out, vowing never to return. She had little money and nowhere to go. They lived in Orange County and she wanted to get out of the big city. She made her way to the port and caught a ferry out to Wildflower Island.

Fortunately for Frankie, she wound up at the Wildflower Cafe looking for a handout. It was the worst day of her life, until she met Tim.

"Excuse me. Would it be okay if I had some of the left over food? You know, just the stuff that people don't eat." Frankie looked down at her feet, ashamed.

"How old are you?" Tim asked the skinny redhead. "How long has it been since you've eaten?"

Frankie looked up into his kind eyes. "I'm…sixteen. It's been a few days since I've eaten. Anything would be fine. Really."

"Sit down. I'll be back in a few minutes." Tim pointed to the nearest table.

Ten minutes later, he walked out with a tray, setting it down on the table in front of Frankie. Her eyes widened at the sight of the hamburger, fries, and soda. She looked up at Tim.

"Eat."

While Frankie dug in, Tim sat down across from her.

"Do you have anywhere to stay?" he asked her, knowing what her answer would be.

With a full mouth, Frankie shook her head.

"You can stay here. We have an extra bedroom upstairs where the family stays. You will be sharing it with Anna. You will have to work though. We need another waitress."

Frankie smiled. "That would be great. Thank you. I've never waitressed before though."

"One of my daughters will train you." Tim stood up. "Find my daughter, Mary, when you are finished here. She'll show you your room and where you can take a shower."

Anna moved in with them a few months before Frankie. She was only 15 years old and one of the smartest people the Carmichaels had ever met. Anna was a computer whiz. She had broken into the mainframe of her high school and upgraded all of her friends' grades. If she had only done it once, she probably would have just been suspended, or perhaps expelled. But, she did it over the course of the entire school year, causing serious problems for the school. She knew how to cover her tracks, and would never have been caught if it hadn't been for the big mouths of teens. With all of her smarts, Anna should have known that. In the end, she wound up in juvenile detention.

Anna was living in Los Angeles when she got into trouble. Her probation officer thought she was a sweet girl and would be overrun by the harder girls living in the detention center. He knew Tim and Roxanne from his frequent visits to the island and thought that Anna would be a perfect candidate for the Carmichaels. And she was. She didn't wait tables, like most of the other girls over the years had done. Anna helped run the office, doing the bookkeeping and other things that helped free up some of Roxanne's time.

Anna was small for her age. She was five feet tall and weighed only 95 pounds. Her skin was dark brown and she had shoulder length, wavy black hair. Because she was so smart, and so tiny, she tended to have trouble with the bullies in school. They found her an easy target, and it made her very shy and withdrawn. This was one of the reasons that she broke into the computer at school and changed the grades of several of her classmates, to get them to like her. However, she blossomed in the care of the Carmichaels. They valued her work ethic, and her opinion on running the business. She became indispensable to them and they told her that she would always have a job with them, if she wanted it.

Anna still had a few months left on her sentence, which would take her through the summer and she would be going home right before school started in the fall.

Mary and Piper loved having the teens living with them. Having grown up at the inn, the twins were used to having the teens around them at all times. It was the only way of life they knew. It was like having a bunch of big sisters around all the time.

One day, when the twins were 10 years old, there were three teenage girls living at the Wildflower, long before Frankie and Anna moved in. One of the girls, a wild 17 year old, named Rachel, decided that they should all go diving at Edgewater Rock. It was a rocky ledge at the top of a cliff, overhanging a deep ridge in the ocean. It was a few miles up the coast, so they had to drive to it. Rachel talked the other two teens and the twins into going. Since Tim and Roxanne were not expected back for several hours, she told the twins that Tim had given her permission to take the car. He had not.

When they arrived at Edgewater Rock, the twins took one look at how high it was and refused to jump. Rachel got irritated and took matters into her own hands. Without warning, she grabbed each of their hands and ran and jumped off. Mary cut her foot on a sharp rock as she fell over the side

When they climbed out of the water, her foot had a deep cut and was bleeding badly. One of the teens wrapped Mary's foot up in a towel and they drove her to the emergency room for stitches. When Tim and Roxanne arrived at the hospital, they were furious at the older girls for putting their daughters' lives in danger.

Mary got stitches, but was otherwise fine. She did end up with a three inch scar across the top of her left foot. All three of the teens were sent back to juvenile detention. It was one of the rare times in all the years they had been taking care of girls, that they sent someone back. The Carmichaels just didn't trust them around their daughters anymore.

CHAPTER 3

"Have you seen Sawyer?" Frankie asked one of the boys on the beach, as she tried to smooth her wild red hair with her hands.

The teenage boy watched her try to tame her hair as it bounced around in the breeze off the water. Then, with only his eyes, he took all of her in from head to toe, and back up again, slowly. This did not go unnoticed by Frankie, whose pinched expression caused him no embarrassment whatsoever.

"No. I saw him earlier, but not in a while. He was over there talking to Alex Spencer," he told her, pointing toward the pier. Frankie and the boy both looked in the direction of the pier. "From here it looked like they were arguing, but I don't know for sure. You can hang out with us if you want." He smiled as he said it.

Frankie rolled her eyes and walked away, not giving the boy another thought. She gave up and pulled her hair back into a pony tail. She loved the natural red color of her hair, but hated that she had to fight with its unruliness on a daily basis.

Frankie was pretty sure she knew why Sawyer and Alex were fighting. It was because of her. A few weeks before, Alex saw Frankie at the cafe and started pursuing her, asking her out several times. She always said no. She had Sawyer, but didn't tell Alex that. It was none of his business. Unfortunately, Alex would not take no for an answer. He began showing up in places where she was…the coffee shop, the park, you name it, he was there. It creeped her out. She even saw him outside the inn at night, just watching the place. He never threatened to harm her, or ever did anything wrong, technically, but it made her very uneasy and jumpy. When she told Sawyer about it, he told her he would take care of it.

No one knew that Frankie was in love. No one but a couple of people, that is. She wasn't on probation, so there was no legal reason she couldn't date. However, it was against the rules of her living at the Wildflower Inn. It was Tim and Roxanne's rule. She needed that job and place to live, so she didn't want to do anything that might cause her to get kicked out. That's why she kept their relationship a secret. As far as Frankie was concerned, Sawyer Hale was the cutest boy she had ever seen, and she fell hard for him.

The only people that knew about her relationship with Sawyer were Anna and Piper. She told Anna. She had to tell someone before she burst wide open. She figured it was safe to tell her, since Anna was not one of their daughters and would have no reason to blab about her. Frankie had no intention of telling Piper, but she found out by mistake. One day Piper was walking on the beach alone, and caught a glimpse of Frankie with her unmistakable head of red hair, on the beach. Frankie was carefully wading in the water to get around some rocky cliffs that jutted out past the water line. There was a secluded beach on the other side of the rocks that only the locals knew existed. It was a closely guarded secret. Rarely did anyone but the teenagers in town go there, for a bit of private fooling around time. They all called it the Cove.

Piper followed Frankie at a safe distance. Frankie never noticed her, as she was intent on getting around the rocks without getting soaking wet or falling and getting hurt. Once Frankie was all the way around, Piper quietly sneaked through the water and around the rocks, to find out what Frankie was up to. Piper knew the secluded beach was there. However, she had no idea what Frankie used it for. Until that day.

Piper stood in the waist high water and peered around the rocks, being careful to stay out of sight. She saw Frankie there with a boy that Piper recognized. It was Sawyer Hale, the cute boy who worked at the grocery store. Piper's crush on Sawyer had been going on for a while. Every time her mother took her to the grocery store, she would look for him. Whenever she saw him, usually in the produce section, Piper would chat him up, hoping he would ask her out sometime. He never did.

As she stood there watching them, Frankie and Sawyer spread out a blanket on top of the sand, sat down on it, and began kissing. Piper could feel the bitterness rising up into her throat. She knew Sawyer was not her boyfriend, but it angered her that Frankie was with him. Piper stood shivering in the cold water, watching them for several minutes, until she could no longer stand it. She needed to get out of there as fast as she could. She picked her way back through the water, around the rocks, slipping once and almost going under, then back onto the sand. It was a bright, sunny, warm day, but just at the moment she made it out of the water, Piper felt a sudden chill run up her spine. She wrapped her arms around the front of her in an effort to stay warm, tears drizzling down her cheeks.

At the beach party Frankie asked dozens of people if they had seen Sawyer. Their secret would not last long at the rate she was going. She spotted her friend, Dixie, holding court with several teen boys.

"Oh hey, Dixie, can I talk to you?"

Frankie took Dixie's arm and pulled her away from the boys, ignoring their glances. They had disappointment written all over their faces. With her short, spiky blonde hair and flawless skin, Dixie was probably the most beautiful girl in school. And she knew it. Conceited as she was, the boys couldn't get enough of her, and the girls mostly hated her. Because it was very difficult to find girl friends, the second that Frankie wanted to be her friend, the two of them were inseparable.

"Yeah, okay, what?" Dixie replied, her drink spilling as she was pulled away from her admirers. "I'm kinda busy over here."

"Have you seen Sawyer?" Frankie asked her.

"No, why? Do you like him?" Dixie gave her a mischievous look. Frankie had not told Dixie about her relationship with Sawyer.

"I don't know. I just want to talk to him, okay? Have you seen him?" Frankie asked her again, trying her best not to show the desperation that she was beginning to feel welling up inside.

"Well, when I first got here, he was surfing, but I haven't seen him since. I've been kind of busy." She looked toward the group of boys that had since dispersed, and frowned.

"Okay, well help me look for him, please." Frankie didn't wait for an answer. She took Dixie's hand and started walking through the crowd. Dixie followed, obediently.

They came across the twins, Piper and Mary, who hadn't seen Sawyer. Piper genuinely liked Frankie, but wouldn't look her in the eyes when they talked about Sawyer. Piper was still a bit hurt that Sawyer chose Frankie over her. Frankie never noticed though, as she was too preoccupied with her search.

Frankie left Dixie with the twins. She walked over and stood at the water line, peering out into the ocean. The surf was choppy that day and the sun gleamed off of the ripples. She shielded her eyes from the harsh sunlight, hoping to get a better look. Was he still out there surfing? She could find no sign of Sawyer and was starting to get worried. Deep in thought, she jumped when she felt a light tap on her right shoulder. Spinning around, she smiled.

"There you are. I've been looking everywhere for you," Frankie told Sawyer as she gave him a quick kiss.

Looking around to make sure no one noticed, Sawyer grabbed her around the waist and hugged her tight as Frankie squealed with delight. Then she backed up a little so they weren't obviously standing so close to each other.

"Hey, how did you get that scratch on your chest?" she asked him, touching it gently.

"Oh this?" He pointed toward himself. "It's nothing. I was out surfing. When I got hit with a huge wave, it knocked me off the board, and I got scratched by a rock. No big deal. It happens all the time."

He grabbed her around the waist, pulled her close to him again, and kissed her on the neck, making her knees weak.

"Okay, okay, that's enough," Frankie told him, pushing him away, and looking toward the Wildflower Inn. "We need to be careful," she said with a smile.

"I think it's a little too late for that now. Everybody on the beach said you were looking for me."

"Oh damn." Frankie looked toward the crowd of partygoers. "Well, maybe they'll all get drunk and forget." She laughed that cute little laugh that Sawyer had grown to love, and he laughed back.

"By the looks of it you may be right. Come on," he said, as he took her hand. "Let's go have some fun."

About an hour later, Frankie and Sawyer were sitting on a log around the small bonfire someone had built. It was still the middle of the day, and very warm out, but everyone thought the fire was fun and it was a great place for them to gather. It was a fun, festive atmosphere and everyone was having a marvelous time.

Dixie sat down on the log next to Frankie and pulled her latest beau down onto the log next to her. "Hey guys, this is…wait, what did you say your name was?" She looked at the boy and waited for a response as she pulled out her lipstick and applied it. No mirror was necessary, as she had applied lipstick thousands of times.

"Cameron," he replied.

"Hi," both Frankie and Sawyer greeted him.

"Isn't he cute?" Dixie whispered to Frankie. Dixie was wearing nothing but white shorts and a pink polka dot bikini top. It suited her.

"Yeah, I guess. Aren't you seeing Alex? And what happened to that other guy you were seeing a couple days ago?" Frankie whispered back. "I forgot his name."

"I don't know. He's around. They're all around." She waved her arms toward the crowd. "I'm much too beautiful to tie myself down to one guy," Dixie smiled. She was only half joking.

"Did you actually just say that?" Frankie asked her, louder than she meant to.

"Say what?" Sawyer asked, suddenly curious.

"Nothing. No big deal," Frankie told him as she threw her cute smile his way. She reached up and brushed his wavy blond hair from his face. Sawyer smiled at her loving gesture.

"Anyway," Dixie jumped in. "Why don't we all go over to the Cove for a little while?" Dixie looked at Cameron, Frankie, and Sawyer with a questioning look.

"That sounds like a good idea," Sawyer replied with a grin, as his blond hair danced in the breeze.

Frankie knew what was on his mind. She had been there before with him and she had a lot of fun making out. But she wasn't even close to being ready to sleep with him, or anyone. As she thought about it, it would be perfect. They could be together, but there was no way they could do anything more with Dixie and Cameron there. So the pressure would be off.

"Yeah, sounds good," Frankie agreed. "But, I think me and Dixie should go first, so we aren't so obvious. Then you two come over a few minutes later."

"Frankie, do you really think no one here knows about you two? I mean look at you. You've been together through most of the party. Believe me when I tell you that you aren't fooling anyone," Dixie announced.

"No, I know. I'm not worried about these guys," Frankie replied, looking around at the partygoers. "I just don't want Tim and Roxanne to see us. They can't really see anything right now from the inn. There are too many kids here. But, if the four of us walk down the beach, toward the Cove, they would probably notice. I want to try to be discreet," Frankie explained. "I don't want them kicking me out for violating the rules."

"Well, okay. I guess. You guys mind?" Dixie asked the boys.

"No, that's fine," Sawyer replied. "Go on and we'll be there in a few minutes. I'll bring some beer."

The girls jumped up, grabbed the blanket that Frankie and Sawyer had been sitting on, and headed down the beach. No one at the party paid them any attention. They had other things on their minds besides the comings and goings of Frankie and Dixie.

CHAPTER 4

"Hey Sawyer, do you know where Frankie is?" Piper looked up into his eyes as she spoke. His tan skin was glistening in the afternoon sun. Piper noticed.

"Um, well….yeah. I don't know if I should tell you. Why do you want to know?"

Piper narrowed her eyes. "Have you been drinking?"

Sawyer shrugged.

"Yeah, okay. My mom is looking for her. Just tell me where she is." Piper shook her head, easily deciphering his vague shrug her way. Her voice raised in pitch as she spoke.

"Fine, okay. She's at the Cove. Her and Dixie are waiting for us. Don't tell her I told you. I don't want her getting mad at me."

"Whatever. She has to come work at the cafe for a little while. So your little rendezvous is gonna have to wait," Piper announced, rolling her eyes, and walking away. The conversation she just had with Sawyer was going a long way toward her getting over her crush on him.

"Piper. Where are you going?" Olivia, one of her classmates, ran up and started walking beside her.

"I need to find Frankie. My mom needs her to work in the cafe."

She had gone to school with Olivia for years, but they didn't know each other well. The two had spoken briefly, every once in a while, when they found themselves standing in line somewhere or when they sat near each other in class. But other than that, they never really talked.

"Do you mind if I tag along? My friends are all hanging out with their boyfriends and pretty much ignoring me," Olivia explained.

"Yeah, I know what you mean." Piper's mind drifted to Sawyer briefly. "I'm just going to the Cove for a minute, but if you want to come, that's fine with me." Piper gestured toward the rocks jutting out into the ocean.

As they walked down the beach, Olivia's long brown hair, braided into ponytail, bounced from side to side, tapping her on the butt with each step. The powder blue shorts and white bathing suit she wore under them, were perfectly complimented by her beautifully tanned skin. Olivia chatted non-stop the entire walk. Piper barely said a word. She liked Olivia, who was always friendly and outgoing. Piper decided that she would make more of an effort to be friends with her.

When the two girls reached the ridge that normally jutted out into the waist high water, they found that the water was much lower than usual. It was only up to their knees. They didn't think anything of it, because the tide changed frequently. They spotted the backs of Frankie and Dixie as they made it around the ridge. Frankie's red hair was unmistakable. Dixie was running her fingers over and over through her short blonde hair, which started to become a tangled mess. It looked like a nervous gesture, though Piper and Olivia could only see their backs. The girls appeared to be looking at something in the sand, but Piper and Olivia couldn't tell what. Piper figured it was probably just a jelly fish or other sea creature that often washed ashore.

"Hey, what are you guys looking at?" Olivia asked as they approached.

Clearly not expecting them, Frankie and Dixie both spun around, surprised that someone had been able to approach without them noticing. The girls turned back around and looked down to the spot in the sand that they had been staring at.

"This," Dixie said, pointing down to the sand in front of them. "This is what we are looking at."

Piper and Olivia gasped in unison when they realized what they were looking at. It was the body of a teenage boy, lying face up. He was covered in bruises and had quite a bit of blood on him. He looked like he had been beaten to death and was almost unrecognizable.

"Oh my god," Olivia chimed in. "What happened?" Her hands flew up, covering her mouth. "I'm gonna be sick."

"How should we know? He was like this when we got here," Frankie told them.

"Isn't that your brother?" Dixie asked as all three of them looked at Olivia.

"What?" Olivia hadn't looked at him that closely. She inched a bit closer to take a better look. "Oh my god, it is. Well, he's my step-brother, but yeah, that's Alex." Tears began to fall down her face. "Is he dead? We need to call someone."

"You must've seen something. Do you know what happened?" Piper said to the two girls that arrived first. She wasn't trying to sound accusatory, but it came out that way anyhow.

"I just told you we didn't. He was already like this," Frankie replied. "Are you accusing us of doing this?"

"I don't know. I just don't know how someone could beat him up and get off this beach without anyone seeing them," Piper responded. "There's only one way out."

"You're bleeding, Frankie," Olivia interjected. "How did that happen?"

Both Piper and Olivia looked at the two girls, narrowing their eyes, waiting for a response.

"What? Are you kidding me? I cut myself on the rocks coming around the ridge. Do I look like I could really beat up a teenage boy? Especially one as big as Alex?" Frankie was beginning to sound very defensive.

Frankie and Olivia didn't like each other much. Well, not at all.

Though Frankie had only been living on the island for a couple of months, she had made an enemy of Olivia within days of her arrival.

One day, Olivia had been eating lunch with her boyfriend at the Wildflower Cafe and Frankie was their waitress. The boyfriend could not keep his eyes off of Frankie, with her curves and cute freckles. Olivia couldn't help but notice. Even though Frankie did nothing to encourage him, and didn't even notice the attention she was getting, Olivia hated her after that. Soon after, Olivia's boyfriend dumped her and pursued Frankie, to no avail.

Over the next two months, Olivia made it her goal in life to make Frankie miserable. She spread vicious rumors about her, though Frankie never knew where they came from. Frankie never was interested in Olivia's boyfriend, but that didn't matter to Olivia. Even with her sweet disposition, Olivia just couldn't let it go.

"There are two of you," Piper said, looking back and forth between Frankie and Dixie, trying to determine if they were killers. "You could have hit him with a bat or something. I don't know."

"You mean something like that?" Olivia interrupted, pointing to a bloody rock in the sand, a few feet from Alex's head.

Suddenly, there was a raspy, gurgling sound. All four girls turned their attention toward the boy lying in the sand.

"Oh my god, he's still alive!" Dixie yelled as she stepped back a few paces and ran her fingers nervously through her short hair.

"We need to go for help," Piper told the girls as she turned around to head back to tell her parents what had happened.

"Wait." Frankie grabbed Piper's elbow to stop her. "What if everyone thinks we did it?"

"We don't know that you didn't," Olivia spoke up.

"What? You know we didn't do this," Dixie retorted. "Just because Frankie and I got here first, doesn't mean we hurt Alex. We found him this way."

"We don't know any such thing," Olivia told her. "You two were standing over him, looking really guilty when we walked up. Besides, I saw Alex and Sawyer arguing at the party. I'm pretty sure it was over you." She was speaking directly to Frankie then. "Maybe you wanted to get rid of him because he was causing trouble between you and Sawyer. Or, maybe Sawyer did it. He was missing from the party for a while. Remember? You were looking all over for him. Everybody knows it."

"There is no way that Sawyer did this. People sometimes do get into arguments without actually killing each other." Frankie was furious at Olivia by then, and got within inches of the girl's face.

"Okay, whoa." Piper jumped in between the two girls. "This is not the time. Alex is in really bad shape and we need to get him to the hospital. We can sort this all out later. If he dies, this whole thing could be a lot worse."

"Fine," Frankie said, raising one palm up toward Olivia. Not breaking her stare into Olivia's eyes, she backed away. "Let's all go get some help."

"What about him?" Olivia pointed to Alex. "Shouldn't one of us stay with him?"

"He's not going anywhere. I don't see any point," Piper replied. "We can go straight to the inn and tell my parents. An ambulance will be here in a few minutes. There's nothing we can do for him. But, if you want to stay here with your brother, then go ahead," Piper said directly to Olivia.

"Stepbrother," Olivia corrected. "And there's no freaking way I'm staying here alone with him." Olivia fidgeted with her long braid, nervously.

"I can't tell if he's still breathing or not," Dixie said, not wanting to get too close to him. "We better hurry."

CHAPTER 5

Suddenly, howling and barking resonated through the air. Everyone at the cafe looked around at each other for a reaction to the disturbance. The music on the beach was too loud for the teenagers to notice the ruckus.

"What has gotten into the dogs?" Tim asked his wife Roxanne.

At the same time that the Carmichaels were getting ready to start serving food for the beach party, Marshall Porter was at the hardware store taking care of some honey-do's. His wife wanted to add a rose garden to their backyard and he was tasked with picking up everything at the store. He knew that Eliza was not really the do-it-yourself type and he would probably end up doing it all. He was okay with that.

"Hey Marshall, how you doin' today buddy?" Dooley, the owner of the store asked him.

Dooley was 75 years old and looked every day his age. He still had a head full of hair, which was pure white, and he was fine with that. He saw no reason to bother trying to make himself look younger by dying his hair. He was at least 50 pounds overweight, which put a lot of stress on his knees. Because of that, he didn't get around quickly.

But, he still got around okay for a 75 year old, as far as he was concerned.

Dooley had known Marshall since he was a little boy, and would come into the store with his father. Dooley and his wife had been good friends with Marshall's grandparents, but they had both passed away almost 20 years ago, when Marshall was just a toddler.

"Oh, I'm fine. How's Dorothy?" Marshall asked politely back. He hadn't seen Dooley's wife in years, because she never went into the store. Talk around town was that she was somewhat of a recluse.

"Naggy as ever," Dooley laughed.

Marshall politely chuckled back at that, feeling a bit badly for Dorothy, who was not there to defend herself. Marshall was not the talkative type and hoped that Dooley would just ring up his purchases so he could leave the uncomfortable conversation.

"So, you got some yard work to do, huh?" It was quite obvious that was what he was there for, but Dooley was just making conversation, as he did with all of his customers.

Because he was the friendly, outgoing type, people tended to like Dooley. Many of the island's old timers stopped by the hardware store frequently just to talk about fishing, sometimes for hours on end. Dooley loved every minute of it. Many years ago, he had planned to retire while still in his 60s, when he was young enough to get out and travel the world. Life didn't quite work out like that.

The hardware store did all right, but it certainly wasn't going to make him rich. Then he kept getting older, as people do. By the time he was 70, he was overweight, had bad knees, and was just too tired to care about seeing the world. The hardware store was his chance to get out of the house and have something to do. Because his friends loved to stop by and chat, he even set up some comfortable chairs and a table near the front desk. Sometimes they would sit for hours without seeing a customer. That was just fine with Dooley. He had the only hardware store on the island. He knew that if someone needed a hammer, they would show up at the store eventually.

Before Marshall could answer Dooley back about his pending yard work, there was a distant roar that seemed to come out of nowhere and felt like it was all around them. It started getting louder and louder, until it was deafening, shaking the entire building and shattering several of the windows. Dooley and Marshall looked at each other in surprise. Both of them hit the ground, expecting the building to tumble down on top of them.

Right about the time Dooley and Marshall felt the earth beginning to shake, the Carmichaels suddenly stopped with their party tasks and looked at each other with wide eyes. The glasses on all of the tables started jiggling and spilling liquid. Tim grabbed a table to steady it.

"Tim, are we having an earthquake?" Roxanne asked, fear clearly showing on her face.

He looked out over the ocean. He saw nothing unusual, but that didn't matter. Tim had lived on Wildflower Island his entire life. He knew what the dull roar meant. He could feel the blood draining from his face, as it turned ashen. He could feel the terror deep down into his soul.

"Roxanne run! Everybody run!" he screamed.

Tim grabbed Roxanne, and ran as fast as they could away from the beach.

"What was that?" Dixie asked the girls, as they were walking toward the ridge to get off of the beach at the Cove.

They had all heard the roar and felt the ground shake and turned to each other for confirmation.

"Oh my god," Piper yelled. "It's an earthquake. We need to get off this beach right now!"

Piper ran for the rocks that jutted out into the water, with the three girls hot on her trail. No one stayed behind to question her decision, though none of them knew exactly what was coming. The water that was just up to their knees a few minutes before, was already up to their thighs, and rising quickly. As they made it around the rocks, Piper ran up the beach screaming for everyone to run. Because the music was intense and the beer flowed freely, not a single partygoer noticed the earthquake.

"Get off the beach! Wave coming! Hurry!" She ran at the stunned teenagers waving her arms like a mad woman. Though many of them were already intoxicated, it only took a second for what she was yelling at them to register.

Chaos ensued. Everyone jumped up and ran, tripping over each other in an effort to get away from the inevitable wave that was coming. They couldn't see it yet, but they knew. Most of them had lived on the island long enough to know it was coming.

Just then there was a large jolt. It could be felt for miles in every direction. Every single teenager and resident on the island felt it that time.

Marshall Porter and Dooley at the hardware store felt what they described later as a loud boom. The entire building shook, knocking gardening supplies off many of the shelves and causing a huge mess. Dooley immediately thought about all the clean up work that would be waiting for him and cringed to himself.

"What the hell was that?" Dooley asked, as he slowly rose from the floor. His 75 year old body didn't move as fast as it used to. He could hear every pop and creak in his old bones. "Did we just have an earthquake? I've never felt anything like that before."

Without a word, Marshall jumped up and took off out the front door of the hardware store, toward his house, leaving his purchases behind. Dooley just watched him go.

"Roxanne, honey, keep running! Go that way." Tim yelled to his wife over the panicked cries of his customers. "I have to look for the girls."

"It's just an earthquake. It's over now," she tried to protest.

"No, it's not. Not even close," he yelled back to her over all the chaos going on around them.

Before Roxanne could say anything more, Tim turned around to head back to the cafe. Roxanne just looked at him, confused. Then she looked up…toward the ocean.

"Oh my god." That was all she could say as she ran for her life.

A few seconds later a large wave hit the inn and cafe. Those employees and teenagers who were not quick enough in their departure were swept off their feet. It wasn't massive tidal wave huge, but it felt that way to the poor people that got caught up in it. There was no escaping it.

The first floor of the Wildflower Inn was hammered. Tim was on the beach side of the building when it hit, and the wave slammed him into the building with such force that for a minute he thought his back was broken. The pain was that agonizing. He immediately lost control of his own body as the water continued slamming him into tables, chairs, and even a car, before he finally was able to claw his way to the surface. He felt as if his lungs were about to explode had he stayed under water one single second longer. Once he caught his breath, his terrified thoughts immediately went to his family. His daughters were pretty good swimmers, but they were no match for the powerful water, and they were still on the beach when the wave hit. He feared for their lives.

When the earthquake hit right off the coast, it was the largest catastrophe to ever hit Wildflower Island. It was very early summer, so most of the tourists hadn't arrived yet, but it was a catastrophe nevertheless. Earthquakes happened here and there to the island, and occasionally large waves came with them. Tim Carmichael grew up in Sea Cove and the wave that hit the town that day was the largest Tim had ever seen.

The water receded almost as fast as it arrived, taking furniture, cars, and a few people with it. No one on or near the beach was left standing. Anyone that could, started getting up to survey the damage and search for their friends and family.

Tim didn't move for several minutes from the spot where he landed when the water started receding. He found himself lying face down, in the sand, with a car right next to him. If that car had landed one foot to the left, it would have been right on top of Tim. He shuddered at the thought. But he had no time to contemplate what had just happened, and what might have happened. He needed to find his family.

As soon as he felt like he could actually get up and walk, gingerly for sure, as his back was still in agony, Tim stood up. He did his best to brush the sand and gunk from his body and started slowly walking in the direction where he last saw his wife running for her life. He had lost both of his shoes and was carefully treading around broken glass and over debris in his search. He needed to find her first, so they could search for their daughters together.

Luckily for his wife, she was far enough away from the water when the wave hit to escape serious injury. Others were not so lucky. A few minutes into his search, Tim found Roxanne, bruised and battered a bit, walking toward him just a couple of blocks away. She started crying the second she spotted him. Until that moment, neither of them knew if the other was still alive. Though it had only been a half hour since he saw her last, he also started crying and hugged her tightly. Any issues that he and Roxanne had, were completely forgotten at that moment.

CHAPTER 6

Bodies littered the coastline for miles.

Within minutes, emergency personnel started arriving. Tim and Roxanne wanted to jump in and help, but finding their daughters was their number one priority. As they searched along the beach, they made frequent stops to help the wounded. This slowed their progress immensely, but it wasn't in their nature to pass by those that needed help, even if it delayed them finding the twins. As they stopped once again to help a teenage boy that was bleeding from being banged up on the rocks, they heard a voice yelling from further up the beach in front of them. They both looked up.

"Mom, Dad, I'm over here!"

One of the twins was yelling for them. From a distance they weren't sure which of their daughters it was. She wasn't moving from her spot on the beach, so they knew something was wrong.

"Roxanne, stay here until help arrives. I'll go get her. I'll be right back." Tim jumped up and started running toward his daughter, before Roxanne even had a chance to respond.

"Daddy, my leg is pinned under the rock and I can't get it out."

"Okay, Mary, let me see what I can do. Are you okay?" He could see a few scratches on her, but otherwise she seemed unhurt.

"Yeah, I think so. Is Piper with you?" Her face was riddled with worry.

"No, we haven't been able to find her," Tim said as he heaved the large rock from Mary's leg.

"Ahhh, that hurts." Mary started crying.

"I'm sorry, Sweetheart. Put your arms around my neck."

Tim picked his daughter up, completely ignoring the searing back pain. The two of them made their way back to where Roxanne was with the teenage boy. Rescue personnel showed up just as they arrived and the three of them left him in their very capable hands.

"Let's take Mary back up to the inn. You can stay with her while I go look for Piper," Tim told his wife.

As they headed toward the inn, they saw someone running toward them. As she got closer, they could see that it was Piper. The four of them hugged and cried as they were reunited. Though Tim was not a religious man, he silently thanked God for sparing his family. They were all alive and that was all he cared about.

Back at the inn, both Frankie and Anna were bandaging up injured teenagers. Tim was never so proud of them. They had just jumped in and started helping without being asked. Frankie glared at Piper, but neither one said a word about their discovery at the Cove.

Frankie was just starting to bandage up Isabella Hale, Sawyer's 8 year old little sister. She had several scrapes on her arms and legs, but nothing serious. She was a cute little thing, who looked a lot like her big brother. She had sandy blonde, wavy, medium length hair. But her soulful brown eyes were what really made Frankie take notice. She was an adorable child and very chatty. Though Frankie had been seeing Sawyer for a few weeks, she had never met anyone in his family. Within minutes, Frankie knew that she was going to like Isabella very much.

"Have you seen your brother since the wave?" Frankie asked Isabella.

"Yes, he's fine. He's out on the beach right now helping people." Isabella looked up toward the direction where she had last seen him. He was nowhere in sight. "How do you know my brother?"

"Oh, um, we go to school together," Frankie stuttered, not expecting the question.

"Oh. He's on the football team, you know," Isabella told her, pride beaming from her face.

"I know."

"Isabella, there you are." Her mother walked up and hugged her. "Are you okay, Sweetheart?"

"I'm fine. This is my friend, Frankie."

Frankie smiled at that, as they had only met five minutes prior. "Hi." Frankie's eyes were downcast. She had never met the parent of a boyfriend before.

"Hello. Come on Isabella, we need to go find your brother." She took the girl's hand and Frankie heard Isabella chattering excitedly as her mother led her away.

The small beach town was a disaster. The beach itself was littered with all sorts of debris. One look and the residents knew that it would take a long time to recover. The locals of Sea Cove were very resourceful though and just about everyone jumped in to help, even those that were unaffected by the water. The morning after the wave, the residents and visitors alike started sorting through the devastation.

Dooley had lived his entire life in the town of Sea Cove and didn't hesitate for a second to load up his delivery truck with buckets, shovels, wheelbarrows, and anything else from the hardware store that he thought might be helpful. The cleanup of his store could wait. There were more pressing issues. He brought the supplies to the Wildflower Inn, which became the headquarters for the rescue and clean up effort. Tim became the unofficial head of the clean up effort. Due to his back pain, he wasn't much help with the physical part, but he could certainly help with the organizational part. A few people started the clean up that very day. Most waited until the next morning to show up.

Across the street from the inn, there was a summer clothing shop. It had been there for many years and Tim even sold some of their items in the lobby of the Wildflower Inn. The shop carried t-shirts, summer dresses, bathing suits, sandals, that sort of thing. All of their inventory was either washed away in the flood or ruined. The owner didn't even bother to lock it up. There was nothing left to take. He would deal with the insurance company later.

The shop became the makeshift morgue when rescue workers started looking for somewhere to temporarily put all the bodies. Due to the cars and other debris blocking the roadways, there was only one usable road in and out of the beach district. Unfortunately, there was no way that they could transport all of the bodies to the hospital, several miles away, in a timely fashion. The shop would have to do for the time being.

Because of Dooley's age and advanced knee problems, he wasn't much help with the actual clean up work. Therefore, he decided to volunteer to oversee the makeshift morgue. It was a macabre job, but someone had to do it. Someone had to be in charge and catalogue the dead. All of the actual medical personnel in the area were trying to save lives and didn't have the time or energy to deal with the dead. They could wait. Besides, Dooley really didn't mind. He had helped out the medical personnel way back when he was in the Army. The sight of blood never did bother him. Once upon a time he seriously thought about going to medical school, but then Dorothy came along and all of that went by the wayside.

After Marshall fled the hardware store he had found his wife and son at home, hiding in the closet, shaking and crying. They lived far enough inland that their house was not affected by the water, but the loud roar and violent shaking of all the houses was still terrifying, no matter where anyone on the island lived. Once he coaxed them out of the closet, and Eliza had a chance to calm down and compose herself, she wanted to help wherever she could. So, the next morning the two of them gathered anything at their house that they thought might be useful; clothing, towels, food, anything at all, and headed to the Wildflower Inn. It was not going to be an easy job. Hundreds of volunteers showed up.

∼

Not long after the wave, Piper checked to make sure that Dixie and Olivia made it off the beach okay. They both made it out with barely a scratch.

Piper and Mary were working diligently in the clean up effort. Their parents did their best to keep their daughters away from the bodies, as they were much too young for that sort of thing. Unfortunately, they couldn't shield them entirely. Bodies were still washing up on shore occasionally, even though it was the next day. The twins were assigned to do their best with cleaning up the inn, and it was a huge job. The first floor was hit hard by the wave and there was water damage everywhere. Not to mention furniture, trash, food, and all sorts of other debris everywhere one looked.

"I'm going to go across the street to see if Dooley needs any help. I'm tired of working on this," Piper told her sister. "The morgue can't be any worse than this mess."

"Okay, whatever," Mary responded, as would be expected of a teenage girl that was left alone to do damage control.

Piper walked across the street to the makeshift morgue, but couldn't find Dooley anywhere. There was no way she was going to go into the morgue, with all of those dead bodies, alone. She was a strong girl, but not strong enough to face the dead without backup. She decided to go back to the inn to work.

As she started across the street, she ran into Frankie. Not wanting to engage in conversation with her, Piper lowered her eyes and started to walk around Frankie, hoping Frankie would take the hint and not speak to her.

"Hang on," Frankie said, stepping in front of Piper. "We need to talk."

Damn, Piper thought. No such luck.

"I know," Piper said as she stopped in the middle of the street.

There was so much debris, that no cars were going to get through, so no need for the girls to worry about being run over.

"What are you going to tell the sheriff?" Frankie asked her directly.

"Just what happened. Olivia and I walked up to find you and Dixie standing over Alex. That's all I really know for sure."

"Are you going to tell them that we did it?" Frankie was chewing on her fingernail, looking very uneasy.

"Well, did you?"

"No! I told you we didn't. That's how we found him." Frankie was sounding quite defensive to Piper.

"I guess you don't have anything to worry about then, do you?" Piper told her.

"Look, right now it doesn't even matter, because no one has found his body. Let's just keep our mouths shut for now." Frankie's desperation was shining through.

"You sound really worried that I'm going to tell someone. That makes me wonder," Piper replied.

"No, I'm not worried. I just don't see the point in even bringing it up. They may never find him," Frankie told her.

"Is that what you're hoping for? That they never find him?" Piper thought Frankie seemed almost hopeful that the body would not be found.

"Yes. I mean no… I just mean that if they don't find him, none of us needs to worry about it." Frankie was stuttering a bit, as she pulled her hair back into a ponytail.

"Well, I'm not worried about it," Piper told the girl defiantly. "I didn't do anything wrong." With that, Piper walked around Frankie and back to the inn.

Frankie stood there, watching her. "She's going to be trouble," Frankie said out loud, looking around quickly to make sure no one heard her.

When Piper walked back into the inn, she didn't see Mary and decided to head to the back rooms to work alone. She was tired of having so many people around, telling her what to do, that she just needed some time to be alone.

Eliza Porter had been working on the beach for two hours when she went looking for Tim. Since he was in charge of the clean up effort, volunteers checked in and out with him. They needed some sort of system to keep track of who was helping, who was injured, or worse, and who was donating items to the effort. It was a lot for Tim to keep track of, even with Roxanne's help, but that was the type of person he was.

Eliza found Tim outside at the cafe cleaning off the wooden deck and setting up card tables and chairs that were brought over from several houses. He was about to serve a lunch of sandwiches and chips to all the volunteers. That's the best he could do with no electricity and no way to cook a hot meal.

"Hi Eliza," Tim greeted her as she walked up. "How is the work coming along?"

"Oh fine, I guess. As good as it can be anyway. It's going to take a lot of work, I'm afraid." Tim nodded in response. "Um, I need to get back to my house to let the babysitter go home and feed my son lunch," she told him.

"Of course. How old is Zachary now?" Tim asked her.

"Eleven months."

"Wow, already? How fast they grow. Before you know it, he'll be a teenager. Would you like to stay for lunch here before you go?"

"Thanks, but no. I'll try to come back tomorrow. Marshall is down the beach working. He's gonna stay a while longer." Eliza waved goodbye as she started walking toward home.

There was a shuttle that was driving volunteers to and from their houses. Without it, nothing would get done, because no one would be able to drive and park anywhere near the beach, where most of the damage was. Eliza did not take the shuttle. She didn't mind the peace and quiet of the walk home.

As she was walking she heard a wailing noise, like that of an injured animal or small child. She couldn't tell where it was coming from though. After several minutes of moving debris about, she found the source of the sound, a little girl about 5 years old, all alone and crying. She must have been there all night. The poor girl was filthy and crying for her mother. Eliza had a bottle of water with her and gave it to the girl who took it greedily.

The girl made Eliza think of her son, and how scared and all alone he would be in the same situation. She immediately picked up the small child and took her to the hospital. They had an area set up where people could look for their missing friends and family. The nurse told her that he would report it to the sheriff and make sure the girl was well taken care of.

CHAPTER 7

"Hey, are you all right?" Cecily asked Piper as she was walking through the bar area of the Wildflower Inn.

Piper stopped and turned to Cecily. "Oh, I'm fine, I guess. Can I tell you something?"

"Of course, Sweetheart. Pull up a barstool. I'll get you a soda."

Cecily poured Piper a root beer out of a can, as she sat down at the bar. Their electricity was still out from the earthquake and wave damage, and many supplies had been ruined in the flood. Cecily had managed to rescue a few cans and bottles from the rubble. She gave them out freely to anyone volunteering to help clean up the Wildflower, and her bar area, especially. It was her pride and joy.

Cecily Blackwood was the bartender at the Wildflower Inn. She had been working for the Carmichaels for several years and was considered part of the family. She was also the town gossip. Everyone in town knew that if they wanted the scoop on anything at all, Cecily was the one to talk to. Everyone also knew that if they wanted their own secrets kept that way, they didn't tell them to her.

Prone to exaggeration, Cecily thrived on gossip and drama, and it was obvious that the earthquake and resulting wave, along with all the people involved, dead or alive, was the greatest drama that had come her way in a long time. She almost seemed to be enjoying herself, in a perverse sort of way. She knew that everyone thought of her as the big mouth of the town, but Cecily felt it was just a harmless form of recreation. She loved that everyone came to her for the latest information. It was how she connected with people.

Cecily was tall, with long brown hair and blue eyes. She was fun loving, outgoing, and easy to talk to, especially after her customers had a few drinks in them. She would always listen, no matter how busy she was. Despite being a gossip, or perhaps because of it, everyone in town loved Cecily, and the Wildflower Inn profited on that fact. There were tons of locals in the bar every night who relished in the stories of love and betrayal that she repeated with abandon. The locals called her 'The Town Whisperer.'

"So what's on your mind?" Cecily asked Piper, as she took a long drink of her root beer and wiped her mouth with her sleeve.

Piper knew Cecily's reputation and thought for a moment that maybe she shouldn't spill her guts to the biggest gossip in town. However, as far as Piper knew, Cecily had never repeated anything Piper told her in confidence. Because of that fact, Piper did trust her.

"Okay, but you have to promise not to repeat this to anyone. Ever. I mean it." Piper gave her the 'I'm really serious' look that Cecily had come to know so well over the years.

"Of course, Baby Girl. I would never repeat anything you tell me. I know my mouth is as big as the Grand Canyon, but I would never betray you. I swear." Cecily held up her fingers as some sort of symbol to prove she would keep her mouth shut. Piper just laughed at her feeble attempt to prove her loyalty and honesty.

Over the next half hour, Piper told Cecily everything. She felt she really needed the advice of an adult, without telling her parents. Piper told Cecily about being at the beach party, then going to look for Frankie, and finding her and Dixie standing over the body of Alex. Cecily was fascinated by the story, riveted on every word. Then she continued to tell Cecily about her confrontation with Frankie in the street, and how Frankie said they should all just keep their mouths shut. If Alex's body was never found, then no one even needs to know.

When Piper was done relating her story, Cecily poured herself a rum and cola and took a big gulp of it as she sat down behind the bar, just opposite of where Piper was sitting. She felt she needed a strong drink after hearing that story.

"What should I do?" Piper asked her, chewing on her bottom lip.

"Wow, that's a really good question." Cecily took a moment to think about it. "I'm sorry to have to ask you this, but did you have anything to do with Alex's death? Please, be honest with me. I want to help."

"No. I swear. I've told you everything. Besides, we don't even know if he's dead. I mean, he probably is now, because he was washed out to sea. But we don't know if he was killed on the beach or not. He might have drowned."

"I don't think that really makes any difference," Cecily told her honestly. "It sounds like he was almost dead anyway. Whoever did this is going to be up for murder. Or attempted murder, at the very least."

Cecily jumped up and grabbed some napkins to hand to her friend. Piper hadn't even realized that tears were running down her face.

"I'm just afraid people are going to think Olivia and I were part of it, since we were there and saw him," Piper told her, reaching for the napkins and wiping the tears from her cheeks. "Should I tell my parents?"

"I probably shouldn't say this," Cecily patted the back of Piper's hand, "but I wouldn't tell them just yet. Frankie is right. They may never find Alex. And if that's the case, there is no reason to get involved in this. You don't need this in your life. It could follow you around forever. Let people just assume he was killed in the wave. A lot of people were."

"I know. You're probably right. But, someone killed him. I don't know if it was Frankie or Dixie, or whoever, but someone did. That means a murderer is here on the island. Can I just ignore that? What if they saw us and want to kill us next?" Piper was sincere in her fear of the unknown.

"Oh honey, don't be so dramatic. I'm sure that whoever killed him, just had a problem with him. He was kind of a jerk, you know. Probably a lot of people didn't like him. I doubt that whoever did it is going to run around trying to kill a bunch more people. They probably just got into a fight and it got out of hand. I'm sure you have nothing to be worried about."

Piper thought for a moment. "Yeah, I guess, but I'm still worried."

"I know. But let's not tell the sheriff just yet, okay?"

"Okay, Cecily, I won't. For now anyway."

Just as Roxanne walked into the room, the bar lit up without warning. They all looked around the room.

"Hey look, the electricity is back on. Finally!" Cecily said. "It's not easy running a bar with no power." She jumped off of her barstool and headed over to resume her clean up work.

"Now we can start renting rooms out again. On the upper floors at least. Well, gotta go." Roxanne smiled as she walked away.

Once Roxanne was out of earshot, Cecily leaned over and whispered to Piper. "Let's not get the sheriff involved just yet. Okay?"

Rex Roberts was the sheriff of Sea Cove. Sheriff of the entire island actually. He was in his sixties, and was in quite good shape for a man his age. His daily gym routine was to thank for that. Rex had been the sheriff for decades, and because of that he knew every single resident by name.

Even though he was cranky and always harassing the locals, no one else wanted the job, so they kept re-electing him. With his alliterative name, he fancied himself a bit of the town super hero, which didn't win him any fans.

Though the locals didn't care much for him, the thousands of visitors they got every summer did. He knew that Wildflower Island survived on the tourists, and he bent over backward to make them feel welcomed. He rarely wrote them a ticket or threw any of the drunks in the holding cell. He wanted the town to be a happy place for people and knew that the more money the town brought in, the easier it was for him to keep his job and make the generous salary that he did. Besides, it was a lot easier job for him if he just looked the other way at minor offenses, like public intoxication, which was probably the largest infraction by the hundreds of thousands of visitors that the island got every year. He liked making things as easy on himself as possible.

CHAPTER 8

The next day, clean up of the beach and town was in full swing. Volunteers were everywhere, which was fantastic, considering a lot of people had their own homes and families to worry about. But the residents of Wildflower Island took great pride in their little piece of earth in the middle of the ocean. Many had lived their entire lives on the island and it was important to them.

"Cecily, have you seen Piper?" Roxanne asked her that morning. She had been up for hours, but no sign of her daughter. "She can't possibly still be in bed, can she?"

"She's a teenager and it's summer break. So, yeah, it's entirely possible," Cecily replied, as she sat down at one of the outdoor cafe tables for breakfast. She propped her tan legs up on one of the chairs in the sun while she ate her pancakes.

Roxanne just shook her head and marveled about how Cecily seemed to be able to eat anything she wanted and never gain an ounce, while Roxanne had to work out constantly to keep her figure. Mary walked out a few seconds later with a plate of fruit and sat down at the table opposite of Cecily.

"Mary, is Piper upstairs?" Roxanne asked her.

"No, I didn't see her. I haven't seen her all morning. She was not in her room when I got up."

"Where could she possibly be? I don't see her on the beach," Roxanne said, shielding her eyes from the bright sun as she perused the beach from her perch on the wooden deck of the cafe. "We have to find her. Something could be wrong."

Roxanne had been wound up pretty tightly since the earthquake and wave. The family knew a few of the people that had died that day. They knew they were beyond lucky that they got out of it with just a few bruises. Even Tim's back was starting to feel better.

"Please everyone. Get up and help me find her." Roxanne was starting to panic.

"Sweetheart. It will be all right. I'm sure she's fine." Tim tried to reassure her by pulling her into a warm, soft bear hug. "She's around here somewhere. I'm sure of it. You know how she is. She's probably down the beach, yapping the ear off of some poor unsuspecting volunteer." He smiled.

Roxanne squirmed out of his arms almost immediately. "What are you doing? That's not funny. We don't have time for this. We need to find Piper." Terrified, tears were streaming down her face by then.

"Okay, you're right. I'm sorry. Mary, go check her bedroom please," Tim instructed his daughter. He knew that he had better do something before his wife became hysterical. It wasn't unheard of.

Mary saw the panic in her parents' faces, which unknowingly made her face crinkle up with worry. She took off running upstairs to Piper's bedroom. When she entered the room, Piper was nowhere to be found. She also checked the rest of the floor and found no trace of her sister.

It didn't take long for Mary to get back to her parents and let them know what was going on. That's when everybody went into panic mode. The Carmichaels rounded up several employees to help them in their search for Piper. An hour later there was still no sign of her.

As they all sat there at one of the tables in the cafe, trying to figure out if they should call the sheriff, a plain looking woman in her forties, walked up to their table. She had streaks of gray hair, rumpled clothes, and a distressed look on her face. It appeared that she hadn't slept in days.

"Excuse me," she interrupted as everyone looked up at her. "I was wondering if you've seen my son? Here's a picture of him." She proceeded to show Roxanne, Tim, and Mary the photograph.

Roxanne gave a cursory glance at the photograph, as she was so wrapped up in her worry for Piper.

At that moment, Dooley walked up to their table. "Do you mind if I take a look at the picture?" he asked the woman, taking the photograph from her hand without waiting for a response. She didn't seem to notice.

Dooley made a point of not mentioning that he was working at the morgue. He knew what all of his 'guests' looked like and wanted to make sure that the woman's son was not among them. He wasn't.

"No, I haven't seen him. There are several people over at the hospital. Have you tried looking there?" he asked the woman, handing back her photograph.

She took it back from him, almost reluctantly, with a pained look on her face. "No, not yet. I just arrived in town on the ferry. Can you please point me in the right direction? Is it within walking distance?" she asked him. "They wouldn't let me bring my car over."

"We will take you there ourselves," Roxanne responded, jumping up out of her chair. "We are looking for our other daughter and want to make sure she isn't there."

"Yes, that would be great. I'll help you look for your daughter too. What does she look like?" the woman asked.

"She looks exactly like this one," Roxanne replied, pointing her thumb at Mary. Mary just smiled, a bit embarrassed.

The woman looked confused for just a second, until she realized what Roxanne meant. "Oh okay. I'll help look for your sister, dear," the woman said to Mary.

As Roxanne got up to go to the hospital, she was not paying a bit of attention to who might be going along with her. She was determined to find her daughter. Tim, Mary, and the woman all followed Roxanne dutifully.

Even though there was a lot of debris in the road, they were able to get their car out and drive to the hospital. As they were walking in to the hospital from the parking lot, the woman, Sheila, told them that her son was on his way to visit her and didn't show up. Since Sea Cove was not far out of the way, and her son liked to take sight seeing detours, especially if he got to ride a ferry, she thought that he might have stopped by to see the quaint little town and the island.

She heard on the news about the earthquake and devastation to the town. When her son didn't arrive as expected, she drove over and got on the ferry as soon as they started taking passengers to the island again. Unfortunately they were all still right in the middle of the rescue and clean up effort and didn't have a complete inventory of the wounded or dead and their whereabouts. Many of the bodies had not been recovered yet. Some would never be recovered, she was told.

The hospital was in chaos. They were obviously understaffed and everyone was frantic. There were people on gurneys everywhere, in many states of injury. The worst cases were dealt with first. There were also several dozen people milling around, looking for their loved ones and waiting for news.

"Excuse me?" Tim stopped one of the nurses walking by.

"Yes, how can I help you?" The words were nice. The tone? Not so much. She was plainly exhausted and frazzled.

Tim dismissed her crankiness. "I'm sorry to bother you. I know you are busy, but we are looking for our children. Can you help us? Please?"

"Go over to the desk there" she pointed. "Someone there can help you." With that, she was gone.

The four of them walked quickly over to the nurses station. Though they tried to get someone's attention, it took several minutes before anyone even acknowledged their presence. Finally, one of the nurses walked over and asked them how he could help. According to the name tag, his name was Nathan.

"Our daughter is missing," Roxanne jumped in. "And this nice woman's son," briefly looking over at Shiela. "Can you tell us if they are here?" Roxanne sounded desperate.

"I'll try, but our records are a mess right now. We are understaffed and have been overrun with patients. We have some volunteers here but are still having a hard time keeping up. I'll do my best. What are their names?" Nathan looked at both Roxanne and Sheila for answers.

Roxanne jumped in first. "Our daughter's name is Piper Carmichael and she's 15 years old."

"And your son?" he asked Sheila.

Roxanne suddenly realized that she had no idea what Sheila's son's name was. She had been so preoccupied with finding Piper that she didn't even think to ask her his name.

"It's George Daniels and he's 24 years old. Please, can you help us?" Sheila sounded desperate.

Nathan looked at his patient roster carefully. "Nooo…sorry, but I don't see either one of them listed here." He flipped the page over to look at the next one, shaking his head. "No, definitely not on my list."

As he looked up from his clipboard, he could see the worry on all of the faces in front of him.

"You know what, let's go see if we can find them. Not everyone is on this list."

He then smiled and led them all on a walk around the entire hospital. They spent about a half hour looking when they came upon one of the rooms with the door closed. Nathan stopped them, and with a pensive look on his face, told them that the man in the room was about George's age. He asked Sheila to come in alone. There really was no need for the others to follow.

"Now before we go in you need to know that this patient is in a deep coma. He was quite banged up by the wave and we don't know if he will ever wake up. We have no idea who he is. Our best guess is that he is in his late teens or early 20s. With all of his scrapes and bruises, that's the closest we can come to assessing his true age right now."

The sincerity that he truly felt for the situation came through in his voice. Sheila was wiping tears from her face by the time he finished explaining the situation. She was terrified, and hopeful at the same time, that it was her son in the room that laid beyond the closed door.

"I understand," Sheila said, trying very hard to hold back the sobbing that was threatening to overcome her.

Nathan just nodded at her and opened the door. He stood back and let her enter the room first, then closed the door behind them. Tim, Roxanne, and Mary stood outside, respectfully.

The poor man in the coma was hooked up to all sorts of machines. One to breathe for him, one to measure his blood pressure, one to deliver fluids and medicine, and a couple more that Sheila had no idea what they did. Nathan was right, he was about her son's age, even had the same dark hair and beach tan skin. But it was not him. That she was sure of. She let out a deep breath of relief. Almost instantly she realized that even though the man in front of her was not her son, he was someone's son, and they were missing him. They were probably frantic with worry, wondering what happened to him. Her heart wrenched for a family she didn't even know.

Sheila looked up at Nathan. "It's not my son," shaking her head from side to side. "What will happen to him?" she asked, gesturing toward the poor soul in the bed, being kept alive by modern technology.

"Well, he'll stay here for a while. If he doesn't wake up after a few months, they will probably transfer him to a long term facility on the mainland. In the meantime, we will put out notices to various media, hoping someone will come forward and claim him," Nathan explained to her.

"That is so sad. It sounds like you are trying to find a home for a lost puppy."

"Yeah, that's kind of what it's like. I've seen it before. We will probably find his family eventually. But it could take a long time. Sometimes people think their loved one has just taken off, so they aren't actively looking for them. When that's the case, they never think to come here. We will notify the sheriff though. He can put out word."

Sheila and Nathan left the room, and the man occupying it. When she rejoined the group, Sheila just shook her head. That's all that was needed to convey that he wasn't her son. They went on their way, following Nathan in a desperate search. Because it wasn't a large hospital, before long they came to the realization that neither Piper nor Sheila's son were there.

As the adults stood talking about their next step, Mary interrupted them. "Mom, can I go get a soda out of the machine?"

"Sure, Honey," she answered back, as she dug some change out of her purse. "Here you go."

Mary took the money and walked over to the soda machine. As she was putting her coins in, there was a tap on her right shoulder. Mary spun around and was surprised to see Harley, the sheriff's daughter, standing behind her. Neither Piper nor Mary liked Harley, and the feeling was mutual. Mary was much less vocal about it than the other two girls were though. Mary just frowned and turned back around to complete her purchase, hoping Harley would take the hint and leave.

"What are you doing here?" Harley asked her.

"Just looking for my sister," Mary replied without turning back around.

"What do you mean that you are looking for her? Is she lost?"

Mary turned to look at her then. "Yes, that's why we are looking for her." Mary turned back around toward the soda machine.

Harley thought the answer was quite sarcastic sounding.

"What happened to her? Did she get hurt in the wave?" Harley asked. She did seem genuinely interested.

"No, she was fine after the wave, but we haven't been able to find her today," Mary answered with her back still to Harley. "So my mom thought maybe she got hurt or something. I don't know. Why are you here?" Mary asked, picking up her can from inside the door flap of the machine, popping off the lid, and taking a sip of her orange soda. As she did so, she turned to face Harley once again.

"My dad hurt his leg while he was looking for bodies after the wave. He twisted his ankle on something, I guess," Harley replied.

"Oh." Mary didn't know the sheriff well, and she couldn't stand Harley. So, she didn't want to have anything more to do with the

SECRETS OF WILDFLOWER ISLAND

conversation. She started to leave Harley's side and head back to her parents, who she could see across the crowded emergency room.

"Mary." Harley called after her and Mary turned back around.

"What?"

"Piper probably just ran away. You know no one likes her right? Why do your parents care anyway? She came with a spare." Harley smiled, satisfied with herself over her twins joke.

"Shut up. My parents are really worried about Piper. Me too. You don't need to be so hateful." Mary surprised herself, standing up to Harley like that.

Just as Harley opened her mouth to say something even more hateful, Mary's parents walked up.

"Hi Harley. What are you doing here? Is everything all right?" Roxanne asked her. She had no idea that there was so much animosity between the girls.

"Oh, I'm fine, Mrs. Carmichael. My dad just twisted his ankle, I think. I'm just waiting for him to be released." Harley replied in her best rendition of a sweet 15 year old girl. "Mary just told me about Piper. I will keep watch for her too and let you know if I see her. I'm sure she's fine." Harley smiled very sweetly.

"That would be very nice of you," Tim replied.

Mary just scowled at her. No one saw it but Harley.

"Well, we have to go," Tim continued. "We need to keep looking for her. Bye Harley."

"Bye Mr. and Mrs. Carmichael."

She immediately regretted doing it, but Mary turned to look one last time at Harley as they walked toward the exit. Harley gave her a smirk and walked away.

"Mom, Dad, what are you guys doing here?"

They all turned to see Piper coming out of one of the exam rooms.

"Oh my god, Piper. Where did you come from?" Roxanne ran over and hugged her daughter tightly. Tim and Mary followed.

"I'm just volunteering here today. I saw the sheriff this morning and he told me that they needed help, so I said I would." She looked at the worried faces of her parents. "Didn't Frankie tell you?"

49

"No, Frankie didn't tell us," Tim replied. "We've been looking all over town for you. Then we thought maybe you got hurt and came here. Sheila is looking for her son and we were helping her too."

They all turned to where Sheila had been standing and she was gone.

"Oh, I guess she left," Mary said.

"Dad, I'm sorry. I swear that I told Frankie to let you know. It was really early and you guys were still asleep. I didn't want to wake you. Frankie was in the cafe getting breakfast ready, so I told her," Piper tried to explain. "I don't know why she didn't tell you."

"Well, are you all right?" Roxanne asked her.

"Yeah, I'm fine. I'm just helping with the paperwork. Mostly getting names and information to help the nurses."

"Yes, she's been a big help." Nathan walked up to them. Then he looked from Piper to Mary. "Oh geez, how did I not put two and two together? You were looking for our little helper here. He put his arm around Piper's shoulder. She is identical to her sister here. I don't know where my head is at today. I could have saved you a lot of trouble. She's been here all along."

Roxanne rolled her eyes in Nathan's direction, and didn't care a bit that he saw her. *How freaking stupid can he be?* she thought.

"They offered me a part-time job. Can I?" Piper asked, raising her eyebrows in a questioning gaze.

"What about your job at the inn?" Tim asked her.

"You don't pay me, so it really isn't a job. It's slave labor."

"It is not," Roxanne replied, irritated with Piper's comment. "It's a family business and we need your help. We'll think about it, okay?"

Piper pouted. "Okay, fine."

CHAPTER 9

Per her parents' orders, Piper spent a few hours going through guest rooms on the first floor of the inn and trying to sort out what was what. In desperate need of a break, as she walked into room 17, she righted a wooden desk chair and sat down to catch her breath. It was one of the few pieces of furniture she found that was undamaged. Everything else was a sopping mess or broken.

    Piper was exhausted, wet, and filthy from her cleaning efforts. She sat down, pulled a hair clip out of her pocket and pinned up her long blonde hair into a giant bun on the top of her head. She didn't care if it looked ridiculous, she just needed to get it up and out of all the gunk and mess. Once done with that task, she turned toward the missing window that faced the ocean. It was a beautiful day and she longed to be outside enjoying it, instead of being forced to clean. She couldn't understand why they didn't hire a cleaning company to do the work. But, her parents were adamant that they do the work themselves. It was a waste of money to hire someone when they were perfectly capable of doing it. Piper vehemently disagreed with their logic.

    Disgusted with the predicament she was in, she looked away from the window and around at the mess she had yet to tackle. That's when she saw him and jumped up out of her chair with a start.

He was a tall man, at least Piper thought he was. It was hard to tell when he was lying on the floor with a desk on top of him, clearly dead. His skin was an ash gray color and the left side of his head was partially caved in from the desk landing on him in all the chaos of the earthquake and wave. It was the most gruesome thing that Piper had ever seen and it clearly disturbed her. She knew that there were a few guests that were unaccounted for, but they had done a quick search and hadn't found any. They just assumed the guests had been out when the wave hit.

Piper felt a sudden chill and looked out the glassless window frame. Most of the windows on the first floor of the inn were gone. It was late afternoon by then and everyone had been working hard all day. It had been a warm sunny day, but it was quickly replaced with what felt like a rapid temperature drop of about 25 degrees. At least that's how it felt to Piper.

With the cold and exhaustion taking over, not to mention the caved in head before her, Piper decided she was done for the day. Unfortunately, there would be plenty more to do the next day. Even though it was just beginning, she had enough excitement for one summer. She left the room and walked down the long hallway to the bottom of the stairs. Piper was too tired and wasn't about to bother going the rest of the way to find her parents.

"Mary! Tell Dad to check room 17! I'm going to my room to take a nap!" she yelled as loud as she could down the hall. She was shivering by that point. "Why is it so cold in here?" she asked herself out loud.

Piper had no idea if anyone heard her yelling, but she decided notice had been effectively given, in case anyone questioned her whereabouts later, which they seemed to do a lot lately. She then headed upstairs to the top floor, where her family lived. They had the entire floor and no one was allowed up there but them. It was high enough that the water never made it that far, so it was mostly undamaged. Unfortunately, most of their things had fallen off shelves, and one of the windows was busted out, but that was the extent of it. No water damage at all.

She kicked off her sandals and crawled under her covers. Piper was eternally grateful for her warm, dry bed. She had to make a concerted effort to put the dead body she had just seen out of her mind. She had seen way too many of them in the past couple of days. She fell asleep almost instantly.

Not long after she fell asleep, a noise in her room woke her. She had been in a deep, dreamless sleep, and came out of the grogginess slowly.

"Psst, Piper. Are you awake?"

It was a whisper that she heard. A voice that seemed to be so far off in the distance that she thought she was dreaming.

It was louder this time. "Piper, wake up. We need to talk to you." Piper finally realized that someone was in her room.

As she opened her eyes, she sat straight up in bed with a start, when she saw Frankie and Dixie standing next to her bed, watching her.

"What the hell are you two doing here?" Piper asked as she rubbed the sleep out of her eyes.

"We need to talk about the beach," Dixie said. "Do you have anything to drink around here?"

"Not in my bedroom. I don't really appreciate the two of you ambushing me like this." Piper was clearly annoyed and rightly so. "How did you even get up here?" She pushed back the covers and climbed out of her bed.

"No one was in the lobby when I got here, so Frankie and I just came up. What's the big deal?" Dixie asked, as she fiddled with one of the long, dangling earrings she was sporting.

"So exactly what about the beach do we need to talk about?" Piper asked the girls, knowing full well what they wanted.

Dixie walked over to the mirror hanging above the dresser and started checking her makeup, even picking up Piper's eyeliner and applying it under her eyes.

"Do you mind?" Piper asked, walking over and yanking the eyeliner out of Dixie's hand. "I don't want to get pink eye."

"Ha ha, very funny," Dixie snarled back at her.

"Can you two just sit down and stay out of my stuff." It wasn't a question. Piper walked over and shut her bedroom door, sticking her head out and peering into the hallway as she did so. Sheesh, I'm acting so paranoid, she thought.

The two girls sat down on a couch across from the bed. Dixie's hair looked different, whiter than Piper had noticed before. She had always been blonde, but now it was startling white. Dixie was certainly someone that wouldn't be overlooked by anyone as she walked down a street. The white, spiky hair, a couple of tattoos, and the huge earrings she never went anywhere without, made her the center of attention in any crowd.

Dixie caught Piper staring. "Do you like my hair? I just bleached it," Dixie asked her as she smoothed her hair a bit.

"Um, I guess. Yeah, it looks good on you." Piper wasn't really sure how to answer that question. Dixie could pull off the look, where many others would not be able to. It wasn't Piper's style, but she didn't lie. It suited Dixie.

Dixie smiled at the compliment.

"We need to get our stories straight, you know, in case someone comes looking for us," Frankie told Piper.

As she sat down on her bed, Piper glared at Frankie. They had been friends until recently, but the incident at the beach changed all of that.

"What stories do we need to get straight? We just walked over to the Cove and found that the two of you were already there. That's pretty much all I know," Piper replied, clearly irritated that the girls were in her room, uninvited.

"Piper. Olivia's here to see you," Mary said through the closed door as she knocked on it. All three girls turned to look at the door.

Piper got up and opened her bedroom door. "Come on in. The more the merrier," Piper said bitterly as she stepped aside to allow

Olivia to enter. "I didn't know you were coming over," she said directly to Olivia.

"I know. I just figured we needed to talk…" The sentence hung in the air as Olivia looked around with wide eyes once she noticed the girls sitting there. She thought it would just be the two of them talking.

"Can I come in too?" Mary asked her. "I already know something is going on and it's about the Cove. So, you might as well let me come in." Mary walked in without waiting for a reply and sat down on Piper's bed.

"Mary, it's probably not a good idea for you to get involved in this," Olivia told her as she plopped on the foot of the bed next to Mary.

All four girls looked over at Piper for a confirmation of what Olivia had just said.

"Well, she obviously already knows something's up. We might as well let her stay," Piper said, looking individually at each girl for a reaction. "We all know that Mary wasn't there, so she can't get into any trouble."

Mary took in a quick breath. "Trouble for what?"

Mary's question was ignored.

"I guess it's fine with me if she stays," Dixie told the girls, shifting her position on the couch, while her gold bracelets clanged together each time she moved.

"Okay, fine," Olivia chimed in. She pulled her long hair back and tied it into a ponytail as she spoke. No hair tie necessary. It was long enough to just tie into a knot without the aid of an elastic band.

So, it was agreed. Mary would be part of the ragtag group of girls, none of them very good friends, and a couple that didn't like each other at all. Piper hated the idea of getting Mary involved, but she already knew enough that she could be trouble if they didn't let her in.

Then there were five.

"What did we miss? You were all here before Mary and I showed up," Olivia asked, smoothing out the ends of her hair with her fingers.

The girls spent the next several minutes telling Mary exactly what happened on the beach that day, and catching Olivia up on the fact that Frankie and Dixie wanted to get their stories straight. An argument ensued about why they needed to compare facts.

"Look, the way I see it," Dixie began, "if you tell people Frankie and I did it, which we didn't by the way, then I will make sure to tell everyone that the two of you were there first." Dixie was talking directly to Piper and Olivia. "So keep your yaps shut and everything will be fine."

Olivia jumped up off the end of the bed. "That's a pretty shitty thing to do to us, when you know damn well that we weren't even there!"

"I don't really care. You are not going to blab and get all of us in trouble for something we didn't even do!" Dixie yelled back. Her bracelets made an obnoxious clatter as she waved her arms around in anger.

"Shhh, keep your voices down," Piper whispered. "And take those bracelets off. They are really annoying," she said directly to Dixie. "If my parents hear us, there's going to be a lot more trouble. They don't need to know what's going on."

Dixie and Olivia both backed down and sat calmly so they could figure out what to do. Dixie rolled her eyes as she removed the bracelets and set them down on the dresser.

"I don't really see that we are getting anywhere," Frankie said. "Can we just agree for now to not say anything? There isn't even a body at this point. No one has found Alex. If they find him, then we can worry about it."

"Have you checked the hospital?" Mary finally jumped into the conversation. She had been completely mute up until that point.

All four girls turned to look at her. They almost forgot she was even there.

"Actually, that's a good idea. Maybe someone found him and he's there recovering," Olivia replied.

"There's a boy, or man maybe, I'm not sure. He's been at the hospital in a coma since the wave. They don't know who he is. I didn't see him, but I know he's there. He could be Alex," Mary explained.

"What?" Frankie asked. "There is? Why didn't we think of that? I'm sure there's a bunch of people at the hospital right now."

"Yeah, it's pretty packed," Piper said. "I've been working there helping the nurses. But I haven't seen the guy in the coma."

"Well what are we waiting for? Let's go." Dixie got up and headed for the bedroom door, grabbing her bracelets off the dresser as she passed it.

"Okay, yes, we should go see if that's him," Piper said, following Dixie. They all got up to head out. "Wait, Mary, can you stay here and cover for me and Frankie? Please?"

"What? I wanna go." Mary was not happy that she was being left out. It was the story of her life. "Can't Frankie stay here?"

Mary gave Frankie a sideways glance, hoping it wouldn't piss her off that she suggested Frankie stay behind.

Piper also looked Frankie's way. Frankie hadn't said anything in response to Mary's suggestion, but by the look on her face, that was not going to happen.

"No, Mary, I don't think Frankie should stay here. She's pretty involved in this whole thing and needs to know first hand what is going on. You can stay, right?" Piper asked Mary again. "Please?"

"Ugh, fine." Mary was not happy about it, but agreed to stay behind. She didn't want everyone to think she was a pain in the ass. "What do I tell Mom and Dad if they ask where you are? They are still mad about you working at the hospital when they didn't know about it."

Piper looked over at Frankie. "Well, I told Frankie to tell them and she didn't. That's not my fault."

Frankie just smiled back. It was painfully obvious to Piper that Frankie purposefully did not tell her parents where she was. Piper didn't know what Frankie was trying to prove. She thought they were friends. Obviously Frankie did not feel the same way.

"Anyway, we should go. Mom and Dad said I could work there occasionally, so tell them I went to work for a little while. Frankie, you should put a hat or scarf or something on. Everyone will see your hair coming a mile away," Piper told her. "We don't need everyone remembering you if the cops start asking questions."

"So. I'm not the only one on the planet with red hair. We will just be at the hospital looking for our friend. Who's gonna care?" Frankie said back sarcastically.

"Come on, we are wasting time." Dixie was standing by the bedroom door, getting impatient.

Everyone got up and headed out of the bedroom, down the stairs, and into the bar. The only one of them that had a drivers license was Frankie, but she had no car. So, Piper asked Cecily to give them a ride to the hospital, explaining that they wanted to visit a friend of theirs that was injured in the wave. The bar was slow and Cecily figured that her co-worker could run it alone for a little while, so she agreed.

Cecily dropped the four girls off in front of the hospital and said she would be back in an hour. She had some errands to run. When they walked in, the local news was on the TV in the emergency room. It was showing photos of the missing people from the wave, in hopes that someone would notify the sheriff if they knew the whereabouts of any of them.

"Oh my god, look." Olivia pointed to the TV.

There was a photo of Alex Spencer smiling on TV. Olivia recognized it as her stepbrother's high school picture from last year. All four girls suddenly looked very guilty. Olivia looked around to see if anyone in the room noticed. No one paid them any attention. She let out a breath of relief.

"Hi Piper. Are you here to work today?" Nurse Nathan walked up to the girls.

"Oh hi. No, we're just here to visit a friend that was injured in the wave."

"Well, what's her name?" Nathan asked as he started looking through the list on the clipboard he was carrying.

"He. It's a he. I don't think his name is on your list," Piper replied.

"Why not?" Nathan dropped the clipboard down to his side as he talked to Piper.

"Um, he's, um, we think he might be the guy in the coma. We just aren't sure," Piper stuttered as she tried to explain why he wouldn't be on the list.

"Why do you think that? And how did you even know about him?" Nathan sounded a bit suspicious.

"When I was working here the nurses were talking about him." Piper didn't stutter that time. She was telling the truth.

"I see." The suspicion was still in his eyes. "It doesn't really matter anyway. You can't see him. We don't allow minors alone in there."

"You can take us in, can't you?" Dixie batted her eyelashes at him. Men were so easy to manipulate for her.

As he took her in, from head to toe, almost imperceptibly, Nathan rolled his eyes at her. She was clearly not his type. Dixie didn't notice. It never occurred to her that she wasn't everyone's type.

"No, I can't. You have to have a parent. So, come back with your parents, sign some paperwork, then you can see him."

Nathan turned around and walked away without saying anything further.

"Now what are we going to do?" Olivia asked the group as she twisted her long hair nervously.

"We are not going to listen to him, that's for sure," Dixie told her. "Come on Piper, show us where his room is."

Dixie pressed the large switch on the wall to her right that automatically opened the large wooden doors, leading into the hallway. She stood to the side to allow Piper to get in the front of the line.

"Fine," Piper told her. "I swear we better not get into trouble."

Piper led the girls directly to the coma patient's room. When they arrived, they stood in the hall for a moment to make sure no one was watching. Then Piper opened the door slowly, peered in to make sure no one was inside, but the patient, and they all piled into the room. The four girls surrounded the bed and stood staring at him.

"Is it him?" Olivia asked. "I can't really tell."

"Me either," Dixie replied, leaning over the bed to get a better look, her bracelets once again clattering about.

"Shhh with the bracelets, Dixie. Seriously." Olivia sounded annoyed.

"Okay, fine." Dixie shook her head with annoyance as she removed her bracelets once again and placed them in her purse.

"I don't think it's him," Piper chimed in.

"No, it's not him," Frankie confirmed. "I'm sure of it. Look at his nose."

They all bent over, staring intently at his nose.

"This guy has a really pointy nose. Alex's is not that pointy. Is it Olivia?" Frankie looked up at her.

"I don't think so," Olivia replied.

"He's your brother. You don't know?" Dixie asked.

"He's my stepbrother. We don't even live together anymore. I'm pretty sure it's not him," Olivia replied.

"Excuse me? Who gave you permission to be in here?"

Everyone turned toward the voice. A woman in pink nurse's scrubs was standing with her hands on her hips. She looked annoyed.

"Oh sorry. We thought this might be her brother," Frankie answered. "It's not him. We're leaving."

No one said a word as the girls quickly made their way out, the nurse glaring at them the entire time.

"Let's get out of this place," Piper said.

CHAPTER 10

That evening at dinner, Tim and Roxanne had another announcement for their daughters. They had decided that Tim would not be moving out after all. Not at the moment anyway. With all the work that needed to be done at the Wildflower Inn and Cafe, they felt that he needed to stay close by. He did move into another room on another floor of the inn though. That way, he could be close by when needed, but not sharing a bed with his wife. The girls were thrilled that he was staying, but understandably concerned that he was not staying on the top floor with them. Things were quiet around the inn for a couple more days.

"Piper, have you seen the news today?" Cecily asked her as she joined Piper at a table on the deck of the cafe and plopped down in the nearest chair.

Piper looked up from her lunch. "No, what's happening now?" A sudden dread came over her.

Cecily looked around to make sure no one was listening. She kept her voice low anyway. "They found Alex's body washed up on shore a few miles up the coast this morning." She leaned forward so Piper could hear her, but no one else could.

"Oh no. Are they sure it's him?" Piper leaned forward, keeping her voice low also.

"Yeah, I guess so. They identified him by some tattoo he has. They are going to confirm through dental records, but they are pretty sure it's him."

"Did they say anything else? Like how they think he died?" Piper asked.

"No. They are going to do an autopsy, according to the news."

"Just great," Piper lamented. "That's just great. Thanks for letting me know."

As Cecily got up, Piper's phone started ringing.

"Hello?"

"Did you see the news?" It was Olivia.

"No, but I just heard about it."

"What are we going to do now?" Olivia asked.

"Nothing. Just keep cool. Try not to panic," Piper told her, as she looked around to make sure no one was listening. She lowered her voice anyway, just in case.

"I know. I'm just worried. Frankie and Dixie already said that they will blame us if he is found."

"Well, that's not exactly what they said, but I understand what you mean." Piper was trying to be the voice of reason. "I hear they are going to do an autopsy. So, let's just wait and see. Maybe nothing will come of it. There are a lot of rocks out there and maybe they'll think he was just banged up from the wave."

"Okay, I guess. I'm just scared that they will think I had something to do with this. I mean, I hated my stepbrother. He was a nasty piece of work. But, I could never do that to anyone. Not ever." Olivia sounded sincere.

"I know you couldn't. Besides, you were with me and I know we didn't do it," Piper told her. "I don't think we should be talking about this on the phone. What if someone is listening?" Piper sounded paranoid, but she didn't care. It wasn't unheard of for people to wiretap phones.

"I gotta go. My foster mom is coming." Olivia hung up before Piper had a chance to respond.

Piper knew her story and understood Olivia's fear. Everyone in town knew that Olivia and Alex were related. Thing is, most people didn't know the real story at all.

Olivia's mother, Janet, married Alex's father, Oscar, when the kids were only 10 years old. Olivia never knew her father. Janet told her that he was a deadbeat, and therefore she never told him about the pregnancy. Alex's mother died when he was very young.

Oscar treated Olivia and her mother badly for years. He was a very violent man. An alcoholic that was prone to rage when intoxicated. Unfortunately, Olivia's mother was too terrified to openly admit to the abuse and spent years enduring it, to the detriment of herself, and more importantly, her defenseless daughter.

By the time Alex was 12 years old, he was several inches taller than Olivia and started following in his father's footsteps. Nowhere near the level of violence of his father, he was a bully nevertheless. Alex picked on Olivia relentlessly, and physically bullying her quickly followed. He would trip her and shove her onto the ground and she would get hurt and bleed. Once she broke her wrist as she hit the ground. Oscar always took his son's side and Janet would not defend Olivia. She was terrified of the backlash if she did. Even when Alex wasn't physically torturing Olivia, he would blame things he did on her, which got her into a lot of trouble with Oscar. She spent years in fear, which caused her to became shy and withdrawn. Alex thought it was great fun to get Olivia into trouble for things she never did.

Ultimately, Alex and his father were the cause of Janet killing herself. One afternoon when she was 13 years old, Olivia arrived home from school to find her mother dead in her bedroom. She had overdosed on pills. Olivia was devastated, as expected. Almost worse than finding her mother like that, was the fact that she was then left alone with the two people she hated most in the world. Olivia never could understand why her mother would do that to her. She left Olivia to a man who didn't have an ounce of paternal instinct or compassion. Oscar had as much empathy for Olivia as if she were just an ant on the sidewalk. Nothing. He didn't care what happened to her at all.

Once her mother was gone, Oscar had no intention of raising two kids on his own, especially one that wasn't even his. He just up and left one day, with no notice whatsoever. Alex went to live with an aunt who lived nearby, and Olivia was sent to a foster family. They lived on the same small island, so Olivia and Alex occasionally ran into each other over the years, never speaking. When they both started attending the same high school, Alex tried to talk to her. He wanted to apologize for his behavior, but she would have absolutely nothing to do with him, avoiding him at all costs.

Because Alex was a teenager, and the injuries to the body looked suspicious, an autopsy was done immediately. It didn't take long to get the results. The coroner determined that Alex was indeed murdered. He told the sheriff that Alex's injuries were caused by repeated blows to the head and body by something rough and heavy, such as a softball sized rock.

"How do you know that he didn't just get banged up on the rocks in the ocean when the wave hit?" Sheriff Rex asked the coroner. "A lot of people were."

"Because a wave would cause a lot of scrapes and injuries for sure. But it wouldn't cause rocks to hit the victim in the same place on the skull repeatedly, causing his head to partially cave in. It's just not possible when being tossed around in the ocean."

"Okay, got it," Rex replied, jotting the information down in his notebook and heading for the exit.

"Wait, there's more."

The sheriff turned around, looking at the coroner. "There is?"

"Yes. There was no water in his lungs," the coroner told him.

The sheriff stood in that spot for just a moment, contemplating what he just heard. He had been a sheriff on an island, obviously surrounded by water, long enough to know what that meant.

"Gotcha. Anything else I need to know?" Rex asked him.

"No, that's about it. Well, as far as his death is concerned. But, you might want to know about something else."

"There's more?" Rex raised one eyebrow with a quizzical look.

"There are multiple healed bone fractures all over his body. This kid has either been in a lot of fights, or has been abused repeatedly over several years. My guess is the latter."

"Thanks," Rex told him, waving back over his shoulder as he walked out the door.

"Hello Olivia," Sheriff Rex greeted when she opened the door to her foster home, about ten minutes after Rex left the coroner's office.

"Um, hi Sheriff."

Rex could see the apprehension in her face. He thought nothing of it as most people had that look when he knocked on their front door. He knew that a lot of people had things they preferred the sheriff didn't know about them. A quick list scrolled through his mind: cheating on their taxes, cheating on their wife, taking a few 'surplus' items from their place of employment. The list went on and on. He didn't care about any of that. His job was to find a killer, which is why Olivia was exactly who he needed to talk to.

"Are your foster parents home?"

"No, why?"

"Why don't you come out here on the porch so we can have a chat."

Rex knew better than to go into a house with only a female teenager at home. He wasn't a stupid man. Rex stepped back a couple of paces so Olivia could open the screen door and step outside. It was a warm day and she was wearing tiny white shorts and a lavender tank top. She closed the screen door behind her and looked up at the sheriff, waiting for him to reveal the reason for his unannounced visit.

"I need to talk to you about your brother Alex."

"Stepbrother, but okay."

"Stepbrother." He nodded. "You know we found his body, right?" Rex asked her.

"Yes, I heard."

"Did he get into a lot of fights?" Rex asked.

Olivia thought that was an odd question and wondered what it had to do with anything. "Some, I guess. Why?"

"I'll ask the questions, if you don't mind."

"Okay, whatever," Olivia said under her breath.

"What did you say, young lady?" Rex was not in the mood for a sassy teenager.

"Nothing. Never mind. Can I go in now?" She reached for the handle of the screen door.

"Not just yet. I have more questions."

Olivia let go of the screen door and crossed her arms.

"Was he accident prone?" Rex asked her.

"I don't know. I don't think so."

"Tell me about his parents," Rex ordered.

"Well…what do you want to know?" It was a very vague question and Olivia had no idea where he was going with it.

"How did they treat him?"

Though a very small number of Olivia's friends knew about her family history, the sheriff certainly did not. It was a closely guarded secret as far as Olivia knew.

"My mom treated him just fine. But, his father was a complete asshole," Olivia blurted out.

Sheriff Rex raised his eyebrows and smiled at her comment.

"Tell me more."

Olivia thought about it for a minute and figured there really was no point in lying. She was too afraid of the sheriff to lie to him anyway.

"Okay, fine. Alex's dad, Oscar, is a horrible man," she began.

Olivia spent the next several minutes telling the sheriff everything. About the beatings, the bullying, her mother's suicide, all of it. She left nothing out. By the time she was done relating her sad story to Rex, even the cranky sheriff was trying to stifle the tears. Even with everything he had seen in all the years he had been in law enforcement, he couldn't understand how people could treat a poor young girl like that. And it wasn't just Olivia he felt badly for. Alex was also a victim in all of it. Even though he had a hand in the mistreatment of Olivia, he learned that awful behavior from his father. It was difficult to fault him for that.

"No one has actually told me for sure how he died." Olivia was fishing. "He drowned in the wave, right?"

"Well Sweetheart, because there is an ongoing investigation, I can't tell you exactly how he died. Not right now anyway. But, you have been a big help and I appreciate it. I'll keep you updated as I can, okay?"

"Okay, thanks."

Rex walked back to his car and left. He knew Olivia had nothing to do with it. She went through a lot in that family, but the girl was not capable of killing anyone. He cleared her from the suspect list before he even got back into his car. Now the hard part. He was going to have to question every single teenager that was on the beach that day. He knew it was their annual first day of summer party and many of them were probably intoxicated, but he had to talk to them anyway.

CHAPTER 11

Piper found her father in the cafe kitchen. "Dad, I need to talk to you about something."

Tim and a couple of employees were busy with preparations for dinner at the cafe. Though, with all the devastation to the island, business was excruciatingly slow. He knew that if things didn't pick up soon, they would be in big trouble.

"Sure, Sweetheart. What do you want to talk about?" Tim continued chopping onions, briefly looking up at his daughter.

Piper looked over at the two men that were working alongside her father, then back at him. Tim saw it and realized that she didn't want to talk in front of anyone.

"Hey, why don't we go sit outside on the deck?" he asked her as he walked over to the sink to wash his hands. They had a strong odor of onions. "Go on out, I'll be right there."

A minute later, Tim sat down across the table from Piper. From the look on her face, it was obvious to Tim that the conversation was going to be a serious one.

"So, what can I do for you?" he asked her with a smile, giving her his full attention. Tim certainly wasn't going to win any Husband of the Year prize, but when one of his daughters wanted to sit down and talk, he gave her his undivided attention.

"Um, okay." Piper was gathering the nerve to tell him. She had decided on her own that it was time, since Alex had been found. She drew in a deep breath, gathering courage. "You know how Alex Spencer went missing after the wave and they found his body, right?"

"Yes."

"Well, me and my friends saw him dead before the wave. Or, maybe dead, we aren't sure," Piper told him as she looked down at the table, afraid that she would see a shocked expression on her father's face.

"What? Where?" Tim's mouth was hanging open. He quickly shut it before she looked up at him. "You need to tell me everything."

"I know. I'm just scared that people will think we did it." Tears threatened to spill onto Piper's cheeks as she fiddled nervously with the long braid in her hair.

"No one is going to think that." Tim reached across the table and patted Piper's hand in a comforting gesture. "What happened?"

"Remember when Mom told me to go find Frankie that day, because you needed her to work?"

Tim nodded.

"Sawyer told me that Frankie was over at the Cove with Dixie. I guess they were waiting for Sawyer and someone else to meet them there. So, Olivia and I walked over to get Frankie. When we got there, Frankie and Dixie were standing over Alex, just looking at him. I don't know if he was dead or alive at that point. He made some sort of a gurgling sound, so I think he was still alive. I was just about to leave to come get you to call an ambulance, when the earthquake hit. I knew we had to get off the beach fast, so we all ran. Then, of course, the wave came and Alex was gone."

With that, Piper's tears could no longer be contained, and she began sobbing. Tim jumped up and walked over to her. He knelt down and put his arms around his daughter to comfort her. He was in shock from what she had just told him and needed a moment to respond anyway. They just sat there in silence for a few minutes.

Once Piper calmed down and wiped her face with some tissues Tim had in his pocket, he retreated back to his chair.

"Sweetheart, why didn't you tell me any of this before?" Tim asked her, genuinely concerned.

"I was just afraid, and the girls all said that we shouldn't tell anyone, in case his body was never found."

"That was really bad advice. You should never hide something like that. If you had told us immediately, we could have told the sheriff. Now, I'm afraid that you girls will all look guilty for not telling anyone." Tim was trying to be truthful with his daughter.

"I know, you're right," Piper replied. "What do we do now?" She began winding her long braid around her hand over and over, in a nervous gesture.

"Honestly? I don't know. Yes, you should have told the sheriff at the time, but since you didn't, I think that maybe you should just keep quiet now. For the time being anyway. Let me think about it, okay? Don't say anything to anyone about it right now," Tim told her.

"Okay, I won't. Dad?"

"Yeah, Sweetheart?"

"I'm really sorry for getting us all wrapped up in this mess."

Piper had the saddest face that Tim had ever seen. "Honey, don't worry about it for now. We'll figure it all out."

Tim spent the next few hours running over the scenario in his mind. Should he tell the sheriff, or shouldn't he? If he did, Piper could be in big trouble. If he didn't tell him, Piper could still be in big trouble. It would not be an easy decision and it made Tim's brain hurt. He didn't want to mention it to Roxanne until he had time to think about it some more. He decided to walk to the pub down the street and have a couple of drinks. It would relax him.

That was his first mistake.

When he walked into the dimly lit pub, he saw a couple of his drinking buddies sitting at the bar. Tim called them his drinking buddies because that was the only place they ever hung out. They never did anything else together. Tim was pretty sure that they would have nothing in common, and nothing to talk about, if they weren't always drunk.

Tim pulled up a barstool next to Jimmy, a man of 40, with a headful of gray hair and a salt and pepper beard. Jimmy easily looked like he was in his mid 50s or so. He certainly was not aging well and the daily drinking didn't help. The man sitting on the other side of Jimmy was Sergio. Sergio was in his mid 30s and spent a great deal of time at the pub, hiding from his wife. They certainly made an interesting trio.

After a few beers, Tim had loosened up quite a bit. In his inebriated mind it seemed like the right thing to do to tell his buddies Piper's story.

That was his second mistake.

Tim didn't realize it at the time, but he was a loud drunk. Even over the music from the jukebox, anyone sitting at the bar could hear him. And they all listened to his story with great interest.

Four hours later, Tim stumbled home.

That was his third mistake.

Roxanne was furious. While he was still at the pub, spilling his guts, so to speak, Roxanne had received a phone call from the wife of one of the pub patrons. He had already called his wife and told her the story that Tim was relating to anyone who would listen.

Roxanne saw no point in getting into a fight about it while Tim was still drunk. The next morning was a different story. She woke him up very early, much to his dismay, and let him have it. Unfortunately for Tim, he remembered very little from the night before. He couldn't even defend himself, because he didn't know what he had actually said and not said. Roxanne was kind enough to fill in the blanks for him and Tim grimaced at his stupidity.

What Tim and Roxanne didn't know was that Sergio, one of Tim's drinking buddies, was also a friend of Oscar Spencer, Alex's father. Sergio wasted no time at all in making a phone call to his old buddy Oscar.

Later that afternoon, Piper and Mary were sitting at the computer they shared, searching for any news reports or other articles about the wave and the people that were missing and dead. Alex Spencer's name was on the list, because his body had been found.

"Does it say anything about him?" Mary asked her sister. "You know, like how he died and stuff."

"No. I hope that's a good thing," Piper replied. "If they haven't determined how he died, then no one can get accused of killing him. So, let's hope nothing changes." Piper tried her best to make it all sound so rational.

"But, don't you feel bad that he's dead?" Mary asked.

Mary had a lot of sympathy for others. It was in her nature from the beginning. She had been a vegetarian, mostly vegan, since she knew what those terms meant. It wasn't her health she worried about. She felt deep compassion for animals. Now she worried for Alex.

"Yeah, kind of. But he was so mean to Olivia, that it's hard to feel sorry for him. I told you that story," Piper reminded Mary. "Even if he wasn't dead when the wave came, he would have drowned. He was in such bad shape that I doubt he was even aware of the whole situation. The wave came and got him and that was that."

Both of the girls sat there in silence for a minute thinking about it. They barely knew Alex, but it didn't matter. He was a human being and didn't deserve what he got. Even his sister, who had suffered at his hands, felt the same way. Olivia never wanted anything like that to happen to him, or anyone else for that matter.

As the twins sat deep in thought, an instant message popped up on the screen. It startled both of them briefly, as they were sitting in the silent room thinking about the situation.

"Geez," Piper jumped. "That scared me. Who is it for?"

Since the computer was shared by both girls, they frequently saw each other's messages. It was a source of contention between the girls and their parents, because the girls each wanted their own computer, for privacy mostly. But Tim and Roxanne refused. They told the girls that it was an unnecessary expense and they wanted them doing things outside in their spare time. Not holed up somewhere with their faces in the computer screens.

"I don't know. It doesn't say," Mary replied. "It's from Anonymous. It says 'I know your little secret.' Oh my god." Mary looked at her sister with wide eyes. "Does that mean what I think it does?"

"I guess. But how in the world could anyone know? We were the only ones on the beach," Piper told her.

"Are you sure?"

"Yes, I'm sure…well…I think so," Piper replied.

Piper sat for a moment thinking about what happened when they were on the beach. She and Olivia walked around the ridge and saw Frankie and Dixie standing there looking at something. She and Olivia walked up to see what it was and then they were all focused on Alex. They couldn't have been there more than ten minutes or so before the ground started to shake.

She wasn't sure at all if anyone even took the time to look around and see if anyone else was there. The Cove was not that big, but there were several spots in the cliffs that the water had worn away over the years. Someone could have hidden there, watching them without being noticed, as long as they were still and quiet. Yes, it was possible, Piper thought.

"You don't sound like you're very sure at all," Mary told her sister.

"I know. Now that I think about it, I'm not positive. I never really looked around to see if anyone was there. I was so focused on Frankie, Dixie, and Alex, that it never occurred to me that someone would be watching. What am I going to do now?"

Piper was visibly upset and shaking. Mary put her arm around her sister to comfort her.

"It's gonna be all right," Mary told her. "I know you didn't have anything to do with this whole thing. I wouldn't doubt it if Dixie did it though. I can't see Frankie killing someone. But Dixie? Maybe. She's kind of a loose cannon. We'll get through this, both of us. I won't let you get accused of something you didn't do."

Piper laid her head on her sister's shoulder and just let her comfort her. Though she was scared to death, Mary did make her feel a bit better.

"Oh, I almost forgot the message." Piper lifted her head off of Mary's shoulder as she said it. "Should we respond?"

"I don't know. What would we say?" Mary asked her.

Piper thought for a moment. "I know. Let's get right to the point."

Piper started typing on the keyboard. 'Who is this?'

'Anonymous.'

"Ugh, that's not helpful at all. Not that I really expected him or her to tell us," Piper said to Mary. "So that's getting us nowhere. Let me try something else."

'What secret?' Piper typed back.

'The Cove.'

"Oh crap," Mary replied.

The girls just looked at each other with fear in their eyes. Someone obviously knew something.

"Well, let's play along and find out for sure," Piper said.

'What about the Cove?' she typed.

'Think about it,' came back at them on the screen.

Then, just as abruptly, Anonymous was gone. He or she had logged off right after the last message.

"I think I scared him off," Piper said.

"That's fine with me," Mary replied. "Maybe he won't come back."

"Yeah, that's wishful thinking. I'm pretty sure that's not the last time we will hear from him."

CHAPTER 12

It took a few days with the sheriff and his deputies, all working many hours of overtime, but they were able to question every single teenager that was on the beach that day. As expected, many of them were quite intoxicated by the time the earthquake hit, making their answers unreliable. However, there was one thing that most of the teens told the sheriff and his deputies, and the stories never wavered.

Most of the partygoers had seen Alex and Sawyer arguing. And the ones that didn't witness it first hand, heard about it right after it happened. The argument was clearly about Frankie.

From what the sheriff could piece together, Frankie was Sawyer's girlfriend. But Alex had a thing for her and had been pursuing Frankie relentlessly. Most of the teens on the beach that day didn't even know that Frankie and Sawyer were an item, until the fight between Alex and Sawyer erupted. After that, the couple showed up at the party together. But the few friends that did know about their relationship, said that Alex would not leave Frankie alone and Sawyer had had enough.

That day, Sawyer found Alex at the party, dragged him down the beach a little ways, and confronted him. Most people could not hear what was said, due to the loud music. But, they learned quickly that

Sawyer was done letting Alex harass his girlfriend. He threatened to hurt Alex if he didn't stop his pursuit immediately. The gossip ran rampant that afternoon.

Once the sheriff and his deputies compared notes, the sheriff paid the Carmichaels a visit.

"Hi Sheriff, what can I do for you?" Tim asked him as Rex walked into the lobby of the inn.

"I'd like to talk to you and Roxanne for a few minutes. Is she around?"

"Um, yes. Anna, can you please go find Roxanne for me?" Tim asked her.

While Anna was getting Roxanne, Tim led the sheriff out to the cafe deck and they sat down in the warm afternoon sunshine. It was late afternoon, and there were no customers there at the time. Roxanne walked out a minute later, sitting down at the table. She gave Tim a quizzical look. He just shrugged in response.

"I wanted to talk to you all about Frankie and her boyfriend, Sawyer," Sheriff Rex explained.

"Her what?" Roxanne asked. "Since when does she have a boyfriend?" She directed her question directly at Tim.

"This is the first I've heard about it," Tim told the both of them.

Rex looked back and forth between the two, surprised that they knew nothing of Frankie's relationship.

"She's not allowed to be dating anyone," Tim told Rex. "But that's between us. Is Frankie in some sort of trouble?"

"Well, probably not. I'm here mostly about Sawyer. Do you know him?"

"No, not really. Just from him hanging around the cafe and on the beach. We've never noticed him even talking to Frankie," Roxanne told him. "What did Sawyer do?"

"Well you know that kid that we found on the beach, Alex Spencer? We've heard from several sources that Sawyer and Alex had a big blow out the day of the wave. Did you see anything?" Rex asked.

Both Tim and Roxanne shook their heads. "No, nothing. But we were so busy with catering and dealing with rowdy teenagers, that it isn't surprising that we didn't see it," Tim told him.

Roxanne nodded in agreement.

"Yeah," Rex responded. He looked out toward the ocean, deep in thought.

"Is there anything else we can help you with, Sheriff?" Roxanne asked, anxious to be rid of him and get on with her day. She wasn't a big fan of Rex's.

"Oh, not right now," he told them, slowly getting up out of the chair. He was still in pretty good shape for a man his age. But, he was in his 60s and his body took a bit longer to get going than it used to. "Thanks for your help folks. I'll bring the family by for dinner sometime."

Shortly thereafter, Rex found Sawyer and a couple of his friends surfing. He stood on the beach, waiting for them to come in from the water, and waved them over as they emerged.

"Hi Sheriff," Sawyer said as the boys walked up to where Rex was standing.

"Sawyer, I'd like to have a little chat with you." He looked at the other two boys standing there. "Alone."

They got the hint and grabbed their things. The boys weren't about to talk to the sheriff any longer than they absolutely had to.

Rex and Sawyer walked up to the wall separating the beach from the boardwalk and sat down on the wall to talk.

"Have you heard about the boy we found? Alex Spencer?" Rex asked him.

"Yes sir. It was on the news."

"I've been questioning everyone that was at the beach that day. Several of them told me about a fight you had with him. Is that true?"

Sawyer hesitated for a moment, looking down at his feet, trying to figure out how to answer the sheriff's question without making himself look guilty of anything. It was quite unfortunate for him that Alex turned up dead not long after they argued.

"Well, sort of. We had an argument, but there was no fight. Not physically anyway. Is that what you mean?"

"What was the argument about?"

"Um, well, I'm seeing this girl, Frankie, and Alex was harassing her. He was going to her work, and bugging her in school, whatever. He wouldn't leave her alone. She wanted nothing to do with him, but he just didn't get it. I told him to leave her alone."

"Is that all you told him?" Rex asked.

"What do you mean?"

"I mean, is that it? Did you threaten him in any way?"

"No, I don't think so. I just told him he better not bother her anymore. That's all." Sawyer averted his eyes from the sheriff.

"Are you sure about that, Son? Because I'm hearing a different story from your friends on the beach."

"Like what?" Sawyer jumped up and was starting to get agitated.

"Calm down." Rex patted the air in a downward motion to get his point across. "We're just talking here, okay?" Rex needed Sawyer to stay calm. He didn't need an altercation at his age. He would not win against an athletic 16 year old. "I was told that you forced Alex down the beach and you two were yelling at each other. Then you threatened to hurt him if he didn't leave your girlfriend alone. Is that pretty much how it went?"

"No, not exactly. I mean, yes, I was mad. Can you blame me? He has been hassling Frankie for weeks now. We yelled at each other, but that's it. I did not threaten him. I swear."

Sawyer held up his palms, toward the sheriff, to indicate that he was not lying. It didn't phase Rex at all. People lied to him all the time. He expected it.

"What about that scratch there on your chest?" Rex asked him.

Sawyer looked down at his own chest. "Oh this?" rubbing his hand down the length of the scratch. "It happened when I was surfing the other day. It happens all the time. There are a lot of rocks out there."

"I see. So when was the last time you saw Alex?"

"That was it. After that, I went surfing, then to the party. I don't think I saw him again after our…discussion."

Rex smiled at Sawyer's attempt to make the fight sound so much better by using the word 'discussion.'

Sawyer had an answer for everything, which the sheriff thought was a bit rehearsed. Sawyer was the most likely person to have killed Alex. The only one with a real motive. It was doubtful that Frankie had anything to do with it. She was frightened of Alex and would never have confronted him. Rex was sure of that.

"Son, I think you need to come down to the station with me."

"What? Why?" Fear ran across Sawyer's face.

"Because we need to talk more about this. I need to get your official statement. Come on," Rex said, standing up. "You can call your parents on the way."

"What am I gonna do with my surfboard?"

"Well it won't fit in my car, that's for sure. Leave it up there on the cafe deck. Have your parents pick it up on their way."

Sawyer ran over to the Wildflower Cafe and laid his surfboard on the deck. Frankie wasn't there, but Tim said it was fine if his parents got it later. He could plainly see what was going on.

"Frankie." Cecily stopped her at the cafe the next morning. "Did you hear that Sawyer got arrested for killing Alex?"

Frankie stopped dead in her tracks and turned to Cecily, while trying to wrangle her unmanageable red hair back into a ponytail. "What? Are you kidding me?"

"Not kidding. My friend works part time at the sheriff's office." Cecily eyed Frankie, as she tried to gauge whether Frankie knew anything or not. But, Frankie was hard to read. Regardless, Cecily was pretty sure that Frankie had no idea what was going on.

"Oh my god. I was wondering why he never called me last night. Now I know. What am I going to do? I need to do something." Panic resonated in her voice.

Frankie was desperately afraid for Sawyer. He didn't kill Alex. Sawyer was a hot head at times, sure, but a murderer? Never.

"I don't think there is anything you can do. His parents and his attorney will have to handle it now," Cecily explained. "Sweetheart, come here and sit down." Cecily patted the chair next to her. She had been eating breakfast when Frankie showed up. Cecily put her fork down and gave Frankie her full attention. She could see that Frankie was visibly upset. Tears were welling up in her eyes and threatened to spill over. Cecily handed her some tissues as Frankie sat down.

"Thanks," Frankie said, as she reached for the tissue and dabbed her eyes. "I can't just sit here. I need to help somehow. I gotta go." Frankie jumped up and ran upstairs toward her room.

"Um, you're welcome," Cecily said out loud to no one.

"You need to get over here right away," Frankie told Dixie on the phone. "I'll get Piper to call Olivia. We all need to talk."

"Okay, fine. I'll be there in a few." Dixie hung up the phone.

When all four girls met up about a half hour later at the cafe, they decided to walk over to the Cove, so they could have some privacy.

"So here we all are again…at ground zero," Dixie said, as they all stood looking down at the spot where they last saw Alex. Dead or alive, they still weren't sure. "So, what is so important that we all had to run over here immediately?" Dixie directed her question at Frankie. All of the girls turned her way.

"Sawyer got arrested yesterday for killing Alex," Frankie explained, as her eyes welled up with tears. She blinked rapidly, trying to stop the inevitable spill over.

"What?" All three said in unison.

"How do you know this?" Olivia asked her. "I haven't heard anything."

"Cecily has a friend that works at the sheriff's office," Frankie told them.

"Oh no. What are we going to do now?" Piper asked.

"We are going to go talk to the sheriff," Frankie jumped in. "Sawyer didn't do this."

"No we are not," Olivia replied. "Piper and I were not even here when it happened. We don't know for sure who did it. If you drag us into this, we will make sure to tell the sheriff that we found you two with the dead body when we got here."

"Is that right?" Frankie responded to Olivia's threat. "How about I tell the sheriff that Dixie and I came up and you and Piper were already here? How about that?"

"You know damn well we weren't. Don't you dare try to pin this on us!" Olivia yelled back.

"Okay, okay," Piper jumped in. She was always doing that, breaking up an argument between Frankie and Olivia. "Stop already. We are getting nowhere."

The girls backed down, but wouldn't look at each other.

"Look, let's just see how this plays out," Dixie said. "Maybe they will let Sawyer go." The morning sunlight made Dixie's stark white spikes appear to be glowing.

"I don't want to let it play out," Frankie responded. "He shouldn't be there."

"Frankie, I agree with Dixie, for now," Piper told her. "We can wait just a little bit longer. It won't kill Sawyer to spend a few days in jail. He'll be fine."

"How do you know? You been in jail lately?" Frankie asked her, sarcastically.

"No. Whatever. You know what I mean," Piper replied, exasperated with Frankie.

She understood where Frankie was coming from. Piper wouldn't want one of her loved ones sitting in jail one minute longer than necessary. But, Frankie had to calm down and let things develop naturally. Running to the sheriff right then was not going to help any of them. It would possibly make things worse. Much worse.

"Did you all get questioned by the sheriff?" Olivia asked.

All three girls confirmed that someone from the sheriff's office questioned them about Alex and if they had seen him that day. None of them mentioned to the officers that they found him beaten, and possibly dead, at the Cove. All of them were too terrified to say anything and get themselves involved in a murder investigation. So, they all lied.

"I need to tell you something else," Piper chimed in. "Someone knows."

"What do you mean that someone knows? Knows what exactly?" Dixie asked.

"I think they know about Alex, but he didn't say for sure," Piper replied.

"Then what are you talking about?" Frankie asked.

"Mary and I were on the computer and an instant message popped up. The person said that they knew our secret about the Cove. I don't know who it was and that's all they said."

"Oh my god," Olivia exclaimed. "What are we going to do now? What did he want?"

"He didn't say what he wanted. Just that he knew," Piper told them. "Have any of you said anything to anyone?"

All of the girls told her that they had not told a soul.

"So how can anyone know? And how do you know it's a 'he'?" Frankie asked.

"I don't know if it is a guy or girl. I'm just guessing it's a guy. I don't know for sure. Is it possible that someone could have been here on the beach that day? Someone we didn't see?" Piper asked.

All four girls looked around.

"Well, I guess it is possible someone was hiding over there in one of those ridges." Dixie pointed toward the cliffs and they all gazed in that direction.

"Yeah, it is possible," Olivia replied. "Did no one think to see if we were alone that day?"

"Did you?" Frankie replied to Olivia with snark in her voice.

"Shut up." That's all Olivia said, directly to Frankie. "We were all obviously preoccupied. Now what are we going to do? If someone knows, then this secret won't stay a secret for long."

The girls spent the next several minutes discussing their options, coming up with nothing new. They had no idea that because of a drunk Tim Carmichael, their story was spreading all over the island like wildfire.

"I think we are just going to have to wait and see if the guy that messaged me does it again. I'm guessing that he will. Let's go. We're getting nowhere here and this beach creeps me out now," Piper told them. "I need to get to work at the hospital anyway."

Piper led the trio off the beach and back up to the Wildflower Cafe, where they dispersed quickly. They figured it was best not to be seen together too much. If one of them started looking guilty, they didn't want anyone to automatically correlate the rest with her.

CHAPTER 13

"Did you hear that the Porter boy is missing?" Roxanne was walking through the inn when Cecily stopped her to chat.

Roxanne stopped abruptly and turned to look at Cecily "What? Little Zachary is missing? Isn't he only a year old?"

"Not even that, I don't think. What do you think happened to him?" Cecily asked her, as she washed wine glasses and set them aside to dry.

"I don't know. This is the first I've heard of it. What do you know?" Roxanne pulled up a barstool to get the latest scoop. She knew that Cecily would know something. Roxanne smoothed the skirt of her yellow sundress while she waited for Cecily to tell her all about Zachary.

It was a quiet, mid-week afternoon and pouring rain, giving them plenty of time to talk. No one was out in the weather if they didn't have to be. There was still a lot of clean up work to be done around the inn, but Cecily had long completed her work on the bar area. The bar was her pride and joy and Cecily always kept it spotless. She was a hard worker, and other than still needing to restock several bottles of liquor that were lost in the wave, she was ready and back in business.

"Well, I heard," Cecily looked around the room and lowered her voice to a whisper, "that Eliza freaked out and was running through the streets calling for her son. Apparently they told the sheriff that Zachary wandered out an unlatched screen door, after the neighbor's Boston Terrier." Cecily gave Roxanne a look that said the story was kind of unbelievable. Not because he was missing, but because, how can a mother lose her kid?

Cecily poured Roxanne a Long Island Iced Tea, while relating her story. It was Roxanne's favorite. She took a long drink before responding.

"Ahh, that's good," Roxanne complimented Cecily on her drink making skills.

"How in the world do you not watch a kid that age every second?" Roxanne asked her. "I mean, I can't even imagine how that could happen. Even if she walked out of the room for a minute, he couldn't have gotten far. He's barely old enough to walk. I don't know if he even can walk yet. So how is he completely gone when she gets back? Something's up. Either someone grabbed him in the house, or she is the most incompetent mother I've ever met, just leaving her son completely unattended like that." Roxanne was getting worked up.

"Right? I don't even have kids and I know better than to leave a one year old completely alone," Cecily replied. "She is very young, but that's no excuse."

The two women stopped speaking for a moment to really think about the implications of leaving a toddler completely alone, even for a minute or two. Did Eliza not know that? How could she not?

"Anyway," Cecily continued, "Eliza called Rex and he took a report. That's all I know for now. I'm guessing everyone is out looking for him. But, with all the mess in town from the wave, and all the people around working on clean up, he may not be everyone's priority. I know that sounds harsh, but I think most people are concerned about their own kids and cleaning up their own stuff," Cecily told her.

"Yeah, you could be right," Roxanne replied. "I'm really worried now. I hope they find him soon. Poor Eliza and Marshall."

Sheriff Rex called for an island wide search for Zachary Porter. Everyone that could help, did. It was easier to get more people involved in the search, because they were already outside, wandering the streets, trying to find their own things and cleaning up. Most didn't leave the few blocks around their own homes though. They hadn't gotten much sleep and were just plain exhausted from all the work they had to do. It wasn't that they didn't care, most just figured he wandered off and would turn up. It was a small town after all, on an island, where bad things rarely happened. It was a place where people didn't lock their cars, or even their front doors. There hadn't been any serious crime in Sea Cove in more years than any of them could remember.

Sheriff Rex was certain that Zachary did not leave the island by ferry. There were cameras all over the port and on the ferry itself and he spent numerous hours perusing the tapes for any sign of him. None was found. The boy could have been taken off the island by a private boat, as there were many of them around the island. Any boat in the marina would have been seen by the cameras. However, there were quite a few houses with their own private dock and no cameras around. That is the only way he could have been taken off the island, unseen. Because of this, Rex and his deputies went door to door with a photo of Zachary, but to no avail. Regardless, the search continued.

Rex put out a multi-state bulletin to quite a few agencies, hoping someone would see the child somewhere and report it. He felt fairly certain that Zachary was no longer on the island. Someone would have seen him if he was still around. It is very difficult to hide a small child and have absolutely no one notice. Rex didn't have high hopes of getting Zachary back though. Small children who were abducted by strangers were rarely recovered.

The Porters were questioned in their son's disappearance, per standard procedure, and ruled out in any wrong doing. The worst the sheriff could come up with was that Eliza should have been watching him more closely. He admonished her for that, which made her cry even more than she already was. It didn't seem to phase Rex. Though he had been the sheriff for more than 30 years, he had very little experience with actual crime. It just didn't happen on his island.

Marshall and Eliza Porter were very young. They were high school sweethearts who got married right after graduation. Literally the day after graduation. Marshall didn't get along with his father at all and wanted nothing more than to get away from him. Getting married was the perfect way to do that.

Then baby Zachary came along within the first year of their marriage. The strain of getting married, having a baby, and trying to pay the bills, all while right out of high school, put a lot of stress on the two of them. Because of all that, they fought. A lot. Not just some yelling, but actual knock down, drag out fights. One couldn't blame Marshall alone though. Eliza gave as good as she got. Their fights were never public though. So, no one had a clue what was going on behind closed doors. In public, they were the model couple.

Regardless of all the fighting, they both adored Zachary, and the sheriff could see that they were devastated by his disappearance, which was why he ruled them out as suspects in short order.

"Are you planning to go to the memorial service?" Cecily asked Roxanne, changing the subject. "They are having one for all the people who died that day."

"Oh, well, I hadn't really thought about it," Roxanne told her honestly. "Yeah, I guess we all should go. We don't need the gossip mill talking about how we shunned the service." Roxanne gave Cecily a crooked smile when she said that. Cecily knew that comment was intended for her and didn't take offense. She loved Roxanne and knew that she was kidding. Mostly kidding anyway. Cecily just smiled back.

"When is it?" Roxanne asked her.

"In a couple of days, I think. I'll let you know when I find out."

Cecily looked up and out the window and saw a large truck. "Oh hey, there's the delivery guy. Finally, I can get the bar restocked. We can talk later," Cecily told Roxanne as she walked toward the back door to let the poor delivery guy in. He was soaking wet from the rain.

CHAPTER 14

Due to the earthquake and resulting wave that devastated the town, not to mention Alex Spencer's murder, the entire island was on edge. The locals stayed in their homes more, where they felt safe. Visitors found that the island seemed almost deserted and still a mess from the wave. Though the clean up effort improved the island dramatically, visitors in general were unhappy. Many arrived on the morning ferry, ready for a long weekend of sand, sun, and shopping, only to turn around and get back on the ferry that same afternoon.

The Wildflower Inn was struggling. If visitors didn't stay, they didn't pay for a room at the inn or meals in the cafe. The Carmichaels depended on the visitors to the island for their survival. Most of the local businesses did. Even the locals didn't frequent the cafe near as much as before. Many were too afraid to leave their own homes, what with a deranged killer and a baby snatcher running loose. Those that did venture out talked of nothing else.

One morning, the ferry brought a special kind of evil with it. Tim Carmichael was standing on the deck of his cafe, watching the ferry passengers disembark, as he often did, when he saw Oscar Spencer step onto the island. Tim's blood ran cold.

Tim didn't know Oscar well, mostly in passing, and an occasional meal at the cafe, but he certainly knew his reputation. Everyone in town did. It wasn't common knowledge before the investigation into his son's death, but it certainly was now. Oscar was a wife beater and he was generally held responsible, in the locals' minds at least, for the suicide of his wife, Olivia's mother. Then of course, there was his son Alex. People knew how Alex treated his sister and others in general. Now Alex was dead.

It just so happened that Olivia was at the cafe that morning, having breakfast with Piper and Mary. The three of them planned to hang out on the beach most of the day, since the twins didn't have to work. There wasn't enough for them to do, since they had Frankie. She could handle it, and was under some obligation to earn her keep.

Tim turned toward the girls, hesitant to deliver the bad news. "Olivia, there's something you need to know."

She lifted her head to look at him. She had just taken a huge bite of her cheese omelet and was in mid chew. "Mm hm," was all she could manage with a mouth full of food.

"Your father…or stepfather actually, just got off the ferry. Are you expecting him?" Tim asked her, fully expecting her to say no.

Olivia's eyes widened and she began chewing furiously. Tim just waited.

"What? No," she was finally able to choke out. "What the hell does he want?" She looked up at Tim. "Oh, sorry."

"It's fine," Tim dismissed her use of the word 'hell.' He was a teenager once, and his vocabulary was far, far worse. "I think you should stay up here with us. I don't want you girls out on the beach until he is gone. Okay?"

He looked back and forth between the three teens. They all nodded. Oscar was a scary man and none of them had any desire to leave the safety of the inn and cafe.

Oscar headed into town to meet up with a few friends. A little while later, he arrived at the sheriff's station, walked up to the front counter, and demanded to speak with Rex.

"The sheriff is not in right now," the office secretary told him.

She was a sweet women, in her early 60s, who took everything calmly. Because she was the first person people talked to when they walked into the sheriff's office, she was the one that usually got the brunt of their frustration. Most didn't have the nerve to yell at the sheriff. It didn't bother her a bit. She would just stand quietly, letting them vent, until they calmed down. When they were done, she would sweetly ask them what she could help them with. It worked very well on most people.

"When will he be back?"

"I'm sorry, I don't know. Would you like me to have him call you when he returns?" she asked him with a smile.

Oscar tapped his fidgety fingers on the front desk. "Yeah, fine." His voice was quite impatient sounding, as he ran his hand through his thick black hair.

She noticed how agitated Oscar seemed as he wrote down his phone number and handed it to her. Just as he was walking out the door, Rex was walking in.

"Rex, I need to talk to you," he blurted out.

"Sheriff. It's Sheriff to you," Rex replied.

He didn't like Oscar. Never did. He had no intention of extending Oscar the courtesy of allowing him to call him by his given name, like he did for most locals. The ones he didn't like were expected to call him 'Sheriff.'

"What?...Oh. Fine. Sheriff then." Oscar understood exactly what Rex was doing.

"Now what can I help you with?" Rex asked as he led Oscar to his office and gestured to a chair so he could sit and they could talk.

"I'm here about my son."

"Yes, I figured. I'm sorry for your loss, by the way."

Oscar looked down at the desk for a moment as he thought about Alex. "Thank you," he replied.

"Do you have that Dixie Bradford girl in jail? I want to talk to her."

"No. I haven't completed the investigation yet. Why would I have her in jail? Do you know something that I don't?"

"I've talked to a lot of people and most of them think she is guilty," Oscar told him.

"Well, I'm not so sure about that. We have someone in custody. We are working on making a case against him. Please understand that these things take time. We need to get it right," Rex told him.

Rex did not want to make the mistake of arresting the wrong person if Sawyer turned out not to be the killer. The town was already losing confidence in his ability to find the culprit.

"I'm sure that's true," Oscar replied through gritted teeth. "But talk around town is that Dixie was seeing Alex and is an extremely jealous person. Have you talked to her?" Rex could have sworn that Oscar bared his teeth at him.

"Of course I have talked to her. I've talked to just about every teenager on this island. You know I can't discuss an active investigation with you." Rex did his best to sound calm, hoping that would relax Oscar a bit.

"Well maybe I should go have a talk with her myself," Oscar replied.

"No you won't. That's a very bad idea. It could jeopardize our investigation. I'm telling you that you need to stay away from her. Let us do our job."

"It doesn't look to me like you are doing your job."

"Mr. Spencer, I have thought of nothing other than this case since Alex's body was found." Rex stopped and watched Oscar for a moment. "Oh, there's something else we need to talk about," Rex added. "The coroner found multiple healed fractures all over Alex's body. You wouldn't happen to know anything about that, would you?"

Oscar's face blanched. That was the last thing he expected to hear from the sheriff.

"Um, no. I wouldn't know anything about that," Oscar said meekly.

"Is that right? According to the coroner, there's no way that Alex could have gotten those fractures on his own, not all of them anyway."

Rex watched Oscar closely for a reaction. Facial expressions could tell him a lot about a person. He had learned to read them well over the years.

"He was an active boy…and clumsy. He broke his arm a couple of times. I'm not surprised that he had a few fractures," Oscar tried to explain.

"No sir, I don't think you understand. The coroner said he had fractures all over his body. It is the coroner's opinion, and mine, that Alex was physically abused. For years."

Oscar's tune changed when he heard that. "I don't know what you are talking about. I'm not aware of any of that." Oscar made a show of checking his watch. "Oh, I didn't realize it was so late. I've got to go. Can we talk later, Sheriff?"

"Yep."

With that, Oscar stood up, effectively ending the discussion, and walked out.

Rex was not surprised by Oscar's sudden departure and was a bit amused by it. He wasn't worried though. When the investigation was over, he would circle back around to Oscar. He wasn't getting away so easily.

"I'll call you if I need your help with anything," Rex called after him as Oscar practically sprinted out the front door.

CHAPTER 15

The next day, Wildflower Island hosted a community memorial service for everyone that was lost in the earthquake and wave. It was held right in the middle of Sea Cove town square and it appeared that everyone on the island showed up.

The service was so packed full of people, that even though it was outside and there were tons of chairs, most people had to stand. The official death count was 27. Most of them locals, but a few were visitors. Quite a few people got up and told stories about their moms, dads, sons, daughters, brothers, sisters, and friends that perished in the wave. It was a very moving service and reduced most of the attendees to tears, especially since everyone on the island knew most of the deceased.

One person was conspicuously absent from those that spoke: Olivia. A few people looked her way, obviously surprised and wondering why she didn't say anything about her stepbrother. A lot of people knew that Olivia and Alex were estranged, but didn't know all of the details. If they had, they would have completely understood why Olivia kept her distance. Piper attempted to get Olivia to speak anyway, regardless of her past with Alex, but she refused.

"Not in a million years will I have anything whatsoever nice to say about that asshole," Olivia said out loud. She didn't care a bit that anyone heard her. "I don't care that he's dead."

"Is that right?"

Piper and Olivia turned around to see the sheriff standing right behind them. Piper gasped without meaning to. Rex glanced quickly at her, then back at Olivia.

"Oh, hi Sheriff," Olivia said, smiling as sweetly as she could. Then she turned back to Piper. "We should go find your parents. I'm sure they're wondering where you are."

"Good idea," Piper replied as the two girls ducked their heads and started to walk away, hoping desperately that the sheriff would not stop them and cause a scene at the service.

"Whoa you two. Hold on just a minute now." Rex stepped in front of them, blocking their departure.

Piper and Olivia stopped dead in their tracks, and slowly looked up to face him. Neither one of them said a word. Piper drew in a deep breath and let it out slowly.

"You don't care that he's dead?" His question was directed to Olivia.

"Well, um, you know…that's not exactly what I meant. You know how he treated me. I was just venting. I didn't mean it literally." Olivia was grasping at anything she could. "It's what people say, you know?"

Piper noticed that several people had stopped paying attention to the service in front of them and were watching the interaction with the sheriff with great interest. She glared directly at them and a few turned away.

"It's not what people say when their brother just died. And especially at his memorial service." Rex gave her a stern look that caused Olivia to shrink back away from him.

"Stepbrother," she replied. Though she didn't know why. The sheriff knew full well that Alex was her stepbrother. She immediately regretted saying it. She was terrified that it sounded like she was being smart with him and she certainly didn't want it to look that way.

"Yes, stepbrother." He paused, looking over their heads, off into the distance for what seemed like an eternity to the girls. "Tell me about your friend Dixie."

"What about her?" Piper asked.

"She was dating Alex Spencer, right?"

"No, I don't think so. I mean, we really aren't friends. I think she went out with a lot of boys," Piper told him.

"Olivia, do you know anything about them?" he asked her.

"No, Sheriff, I don't. Alex and I don't...well didn't, talk. We haven't in a long time."

"Is she the jealous type? From what I understand, Alex had a serious crush on your friend Frankie," Rex asked.

The girls looked at each other for a moment, which did not go unnoticed by Rex.

"Honestly, we don't know, Sheriff," Piper responded. "She hasn't talked much to us about Alex. Like I said, we aren't really friends."

"I see. We will talk more later, but for now, you two can go."

Piper and Olivia took off like a shot. They had no intention of standing there with the sheriff one second longer than they needed to. He watched them as they left.

At that moment, Oscar stepped off the stage after his heart-warming speech about his son. There wasn't a dry eye in the place when he stepped down. As he reached the bottom of the stairs, he had his head bent down and was wiping the tears from his face, not paying attention to where he was going. He ran smack into Dixie, who was looking for her friends and also not paying attention to anyone in front of her.

"Oh, sorry...oh it's you," Oscar said when he looked up and saw who it was.

Dixie instinctively reached up to rub her left shoulder where it had met Oscar's left shoulder, with a thud.

"Oh, hi Mr. Spencer. I'm really sorry about your son."

"I'll bet you are." Sarcasm dripped from his voice.

"What?" she asked. "What does that mean?"

"I know you are the one that killed my son. I just have to prove it."

"Me? No sir. I didn't kill him. I don't know who did." Dixie's bright white hair sparkled in the sunlight.

Dixie was taken aback by the accusation. She looked around to see who was listening. A few people were definitely interested in their conversation. Oscar also noticed the gathering crowd.

He leaned forward and whispered into her ear. "We'll talk later," he hissed. "You are not getting away with this."

Dixie stepped back away from him and his threat. She watched him as he walked away, never looking back.

Piper and Olivia were standing together talking, right after the memorial service, when Olivia felt a tug on her long ponytail. She spun around to face a group of teenage boys.

"You know, Sawyer is a buddy of mine and he didn't kill your damn brother."

A boy named Matt confronted Olivia. She didn't know him personally and had only seen him hanging out with Sawyer a few times. He was with a couple of his friends, who stood there quietly, trying to look mean. It really didn't work.

"Just leave her alone, Matt," Frankie told him as she and Dixie walked up to talk to Piper and Olivia. "It's not Olivia's fault that the sheriff arrested Sawyer."

"What? Are you on her side now?" Matt was confrontational with Frankie and she was in no mood.

"What side is that? I'm just trying to get through this while the sheriff figures out who did it. Go away."

Frankie waved the back of her hands at him in a shooing gesture. The three boys smirked at Frankie and walked away.

"Nice one, Frankie," Dixie told her, smiling. "I can see why Alex liked you."

All three girls looked at Dixie, confused by her comment.

"What is that supposed to mean?" Frankie asked her.

"You know." Dixie gave her a knowing look.

"No, I don't know," Frankie replied. "Maybe you can be more

specific."

"I'm talking about Alex liking you. He was always following you around and stuff. You know, whatever."

Dixie tried her best to make her comments sound innocuous, but it wasn't working. She immediately regretted saying it. It was obvious to her that either Frankie didn't know that Alex liked her, or she didn't know that anyone else knew. Either one was not going to work out well for Dixie. She knew right away that she should never have brought it up.

"You know what? Never mind. I'm an idiot and don't know what I'm talking about." It was Dixie's feeble attempt at calming the situation and changing the subject. She began twisting her spiky hair out of nervousness.

"What the hell?" Piper exclaimed. "The sheriff just told Olivia and me that you were dating Alex. We didn't really believe him. Is this how you know about him and Frankie?"

"Wait a minute," Frankie jumped in. "There is no Alex and me. I don't know where that even came from."

"That's not what I meant," Piper replied. "Was he really following you around? Like some sort of stalker?" she asked Frankie.

Frankie lowered her eyes. She really didn't want people knowing about that, but it was too late. She looked up at all the girls. "Yeah, he was. He was stalking me, I guess. Sawyer knew and tried to get him to leave me alone, and he ended up getting arrested. All because of me."

"No, it wasn't your fault," Olivia told her. "Alex was a pathetic human being. He bullied me, cheated on Dixie here," she said, gesturing toward Dixie, "and he stalked Frankie." She turned to look at Piper. "And you know my story. Every horrible detail."

Piper nodded. As they all stood thinking about Alex, they all realized that they had motive. Every one of them. They all hated Alex, and they knew it. Each girl was terrified that someone would figure out that each of them had a reason to kill Alex.

"Did you do this, Dixie? Did you kill my stepbrother?" Olivia asked her directly.

All three girls looked directly at Dixie, arms crossed tightly against their bodies. Suspicion written on their faces.

Dixie looked directly into the eyes of each girl. "What? No, I didn't do it. Yes I was seeing him, but so what? He wasn't the only one I was seeing. I don't care if he liked Frankie. He could date anyone he wanted. It didn't matter to me."

"Really? Well you know what I think?" Olivia told them. "I think you were pissed off that my stepbrother had a thing for Frankie and you killed him."

"Are you freaking kidding me? Even if I was pissed, which I wasn't, I wouldn't kill him. I couldn't do that." Dixie was trying desperately to defend herself from the sudden accusations flying her way.

Dixie looked as if she was going to start crying. She felt ganged up on by the girls. Girls she thought were her friends. Sort of friends, anyway. They had all been in this predicament together and she thought they were bonding. How wrong she was.

"Besides, my friends don't think I did it. I guess you aren't my friends," Dixie announced.

"What?!" Piper exclaimed. "You told people? What exactly did you tell them?"

"Um, nothing. I mean I just told them about us finding Alex there," Dixie replied.

"Oh my god, you are so stupid," Olivia jumped in. "Why would you tell people?"

"Seriously, what difference does it make? We found him that way. What's the big deal?" Dixie replied, pulling out her compact and checking her makeup.

"You just aren't taking this whole mess seriously, are you Dixie?" Frankie asked her. "People are going to think we did it, if you keep talking to them about it."

"No they aren't. Don't be so dramatic," Dixie replied. She had calmed way down and was no longer in danger of breaking down in tears. At that point, she was just getting angry.

"Do you not understand that we could all go to jail?" Piper chimed in.

"For what? We didn't do it!" Dixie yelled.

Dixie had had enough of the third degree. She turned around and stormed away without another word to the group. She had put her time in at the memorial service, and just wanted out of there.

"Now that she is gone, we need to figure out what to do about her," Piper told the other two remaining girls.

"You don't really think she killed Alex, do you?" Olivia asked the girls.

"At this point, I don't know anything," Frankie replied. "I wasn't with her all day at the party. She could have met Alex at the Cove before we walked over there. But then again, anyone could have. I just don't know."

"Well, let's keep a close eye on her. If it's her, she could be dangerous," Piper suggested to the other two.

"I'm certain that Sawyer had nothing to do with this," Frankie said. "I haven't told anyone anything, of course, but when I talk to people, everybody says that they like him. He has tons of friends. Even though he got arrested, I don't think anyone thinks he killed Alex. Most people didn't like Alex. There are probably a lot of people around the island with motive."

"Hey," Mary said as she walked up and joined the three girls.

"Hi Mary," they all replied.

"Where are Mom and Dad?" Piper asked her.

"They went home. I figured I would hang out with you guys," Mary told them. "I need to tell you something."

"About what?" Olivia asked.

"It's about Dixie," Mary started. "I just heard her talking to a couple of people. She told them she was mad at Alex for cheating on her. Then she told them that her and some girls, she didn't say it was you guys, found Alex beaten on the beach at the Cove. Do you think maybe she killed him?"

"That's exactly what we were just talking about," Piper replied. "We are starting to wonder about her."

"Yeah, we have no idea if she is guilty, or just too stupid to keep her big mouth shut," Frankie said. "She always wants to be the center of attention, and this is working for her."

CHAPTER 16

By the next morning, the entire thing was getting out of hand. The locals talked of nothing but Alex's murder and who they thought was responsible. Quite a few people heard that Alex and Dixie were dating, and about Alex cheating on her. That was a perfect motive, as far as they were concerned. It certainly was not unheard of for a scorned person to commit such a crime, though not usually by someone so young.

Others decided that it had to be one of The Wildflowers, the town's affectionate nickname for the troubled teens that lived and worked at the Wildflower Inn. Since Anna was quiet and kept mostly to herself, Frankie was at the top of everyone's list. Since the beach party, it had come to be common knowledge that she and Sawyer were an item, and that Alex was harassing her. Since Sawyer was so well liked, Frankie was the one they decided must be guilty.

Those that thought Frankie was the responsible party, treated her as if she were guilty, with no proof whatsoever. Business at the Wildflower Cafe suffered because of it. Though the cafe was a favorite among the locals, those people stayed away, not wanting to have anything to do with Frankie or the place where she lived and worked.

When someone did run across Frankie somewhere, they either turned and walked in the other direction, avoiding her completely, or confronted her. Many days, Frankie arrived home to the inn in tears. Though she was not normally a shrinking violet, she couldn't stand up to groups of people accosting her. Rarely did anyone do so alone, because people are generally cowards. They would use the group mentality to harass a poor teenager, who could not defend herself alone.

"Hello Frankie," Sheriff Rex greeted her as he walked into the Wildflower Inn.

"Hi Sheriff."

"Can you please find the Carmichaels for me? Tell them I would like to speak with them and Piper. You need to be part of the conversation too."

Frankie raised her eyebrows questioningly, but the sheriff did not elaborate. "Okay," she responded, as she turned to get everyone.

Rex walked outside to the cafe and sat down at one of the tables, closest to the ocean. Though he didn't spend much time on the beach anymore, he loved sitting and watching the waves. It was one of his favorite past times.

Two minutes later, Tim, Roxanne, Piper, and Frankie joined him at the table.

"What can we do for you, Sheriff? Would you like something to eat or drink?" Tim asked as he greeted Rex with a handshake and sat down.

"No. Thank you anyway. I need to ask these young ladies here a few questions, if you don't mind," Rex replied.

"Do we need a lawyer?" Roxanne asked. She didn't intend it to sound confrontational.

"You are certainly within your rights to have one present. But honestly, I'm just here as part of my investigation into Alex Spencer's death and just want to talk. No one is being accused of anything right now," Rex replied.

The last thing he wanted was to have to deal with attorneys. They tended to make his job harder because people were not free to just answer his questions in the casual atmosphere that he preferred. He waited while Tim and Roxanne discussed the matter quietly.

"All right, that's fine. Go ahead and ask your questions, Sheriff," Roxanne told him.

Rex smiled slightly as he picked up his notepad to consult it.

"I've been talking with the kids again who were at the beach party that day. Many were hesitant to say anything right after Alex's body was discovered. But, things have calmed down a bit and many were a bit more forthcoming this time." He paused for a moment, before he continued.

"Several of the kids have told me that they saw you and Piper, along with Dixie Bradford and Olivia Garrett, running from the Cove right before the wave hit. Is that true?" he asked Frankie directly, as he glanced back and forth to each girl.

Frankie and Piper looked over at each other. The three adults could see the looks on their faces, as they turned away quickly from each other.

"No, it's not what you think," Piper replied.

"So you weren't running from the Cove, like I was told?" Rex asked Piper.

"No. I mean yes, we were running from there. But, not because of what you think. It was because the wave was coming and we needed to warn people," Piper tried to explain.

Frankie kept her mouth shut, as she happily let Piper do all the talking.

"So what do I think?" Rex asked her.

Piper hesitated a moment, not sure what he did and didn't know. Should she say that they found Alex on the beach like that? Should she wait and see if he knew already? She glanced up to see Mary standing in the doorway between the inn and cafe, watching and listening. Mary shook her head back and forth, ever so slightly. Mary was the more rational of the two. She always thought things out before doing or saying anything. Piper understood what Mary was telling her.

"I really don't know what you think. You said you were here investigating Alex's death. I thought that had something to do with your question." Piper tried to reel in her previous answer.

"I see." Rex looked out over the ocean while he thought about his next question. "What were the four of you doing on that beach?"

Piper looked at her parents. "Um, nothing really." That was all Piper wanted to say.

"Nothing?" Rex asked her. "Care to expand on that? Frankie, you've been conspicuously quiet. You have anything to say?"

"No sir. We weren't doing anything," Frankie told him. "We were at the party and went for a walk, that's all."

"The four of you? By all accounts, you four girls aren't even friends. Why would you go for a walk together?" Rex asked. He wasn't buying it.

"Girls, if there is anything that the sheriff needs to know, then tell him," Tim ordered.

"We didn't do anything," Frankie told them.

Piper gave her a look. Rex saw it. He didn't miss much.

"No one said you did," Rex told her. "I do have to say though, it looks like the two of you aren't telling me everything. I know more than you think, so it would be in your best interest to tell me the truth. All of it."

"Piper, Frankie, tell him everything you know," Roxanne finally chimed in. "If you are hiding anything, you will get into a lot more trouble later." She gave them the 'I'm really serious' face.

"Okay, fine, we'll tell you," Piper said to the sheriff.

Piper had wanted to tell from the beginning, but was talked out of it by her well meaning 'friends,' and Cecily, an adult that should have given her better advice. She didn't want to lie anymore. She wanted it to just all end. The lies, the hiding, the meeting in secret, all of it.

"Piper...," Frankie said with widened eyes.

"No, it's fine," Piper interrupted her. "I'm tired of all the lying and deceit. I just want this to be over with."

Piper told the sheriff everything. She told him how she and Olivia walked over to the Cove, to find Frankie, because she was needed at the cafe, and how they found Frankie and Dixie there already with

Alex. She told him that Alex was badly beaten and they weren't even sure if he was still alive at that point or not. Then the earthquake happened and they ran. That was all she knew for sure. She told the sheriff that he would have to get the rest of the story from Frankie. She looked over at Frankie as she said that. Frankie didn't look very happy, but Piper didn't care. She felt better already, as if a car had been lifted off her chest.

Frankie corroborated Piper's story, adding in the part where she and Dixie found Alex and the state they found him in.

Piper and Frankie had no idea that the sheriff already knew that the four girls found Alex already beaten at the Cove and were keeping that fact from him. He wanted to hear it directly from them, not from some teenagers that had heard it through the fast moving gossip train on the island.

"Frankie, were you seeing Alex Spencer?" Rex asked her.

"God no. Never," Frankie said a bit too quickly.

"Why such a strong reaction? Didn't you like Alex?" he asked her.

"Um, no." Frankie hesitated, not wanting to sound too anxious. "He was stalking me."

"Is that right? Sounds like motive to me," Rex replied.

"No, Sheriff. I just wanted him to leave me alone. I didn't want him to die," Frankie told him.

"How about your boyfriend? Did Sawyer want him dead for what he was doing?"

"No. Sawyer told him to leave me alone. That's all. Sawyer didn't do it. I swear," Frankie replied.

Rex just smiled at her comment. It never failed that someone would tell him something and swear directly to him that they were telling the truth. Sure you are, he always thought.

"Tell me about your friend, Dixie, and her relationship with Alex."

"Well, I found out they were dating long after the wave. I had no idea before," Frankie explained. "Dixie dated a lot of boys. She loves being the center of attention and that's how she gets it. Look, I like Dixie, but she doesn't really have the brains to kill someone, even at the spur of the moment. She's more of the type that would complain about it to other boys and let them take care of it. She's not a killer. Besides, she can't weigh more than 100 pounds. There's no way she could beat Alex like that. She just doesn't have the juice."

Rex smiled at her comment.

"You'd be surprised what someone can do if they are angry enough. I've seen it happen before," Rex told her. "That's enough for today. I'll probably have more questions for you later. Mr. and Mrs. Carmichael, thank you for your time."

Rex stood up and left.

CHAPTER 17

After dinner, Tim and Roxanne took a walk down the main street of town just to get away for a while. The stress of Piper and her involvement in the investigation into Alex Spencer's death, as well as the ongoing clean up and restoration of the town after the wave, was getting to both of them. They sat down on a concrete bench, drinking strawberry smoothies, while they watched the waves.

"So, what are we going to do about Piper?" Tim asked his wife.

"That's a really good question." It was the best answer Roxanne could come up with.

"Maybe we should get a lawyer," Tim suggested, as he turned to look at his wife. "And then there's Frankie. Should we get one for her too?"

"Not right now. I don't think Piper is a suspect at all. At least I certainly hope not. Frankie? I'm not so sure. Piper's not lying. We did send her to go get Frankie that day. So we know she wasn't there when it happened," Roxanne said matter-of-factly.

Tim shook his head. "We don't know that for sure. We don't even know what time it happened. He could have been lying there for hours for all we know. We don't know for a fact that she is not involved."

"My daughter is not a killer! I'm not going to believe for a second that she is! How can you say that!" Roxanne stood up abruptly, knocking her smoothie all over Tim's shorts and bare legs.

Tim jumped up from the shock of the ice cold liquid on his legs. "What the hell, Roxanne?! Just calm down!"

Roxanne completely ignored the fact that she just spilled her smoothie all over him, and started walking away.

"Roxanne!" Tim called after her. He was trying to wipe off his shorts and legs with a napkin as he ran after her. It looked like some strange run, hop, dance thing to anyone watching him.

"Roxanne, stop!" he yelled again.

She stopped abruptly, and turned toward him. "What?" Roxanne refused to make eye contact, pressing her lips together.

"Why do you look so irritated with me? I was just trying to have a conversation with you."

"Because I don't want people thinking my daughter had anything to do with this. That's why I'm irritated," Roxanne replied, as she looked him in the eyes, then down to his soggy shorts and pink stained legs.

"Stop saying 'my daughter.' She's our daughter. And what about Mary? Do you think she's involved at all?" Tim asked.

"How should I know? No one has mentioned her name, so we should just try our best to leave her out of it. For now, at least. The sheriff hasn't brought up Mary's name at all," Roxanne replied.

"Those girls don't do much that the other one doesn't know about," Tim replied. "Even if Mary wasn't there, she probably knows all about it."

"Why are you trying to get Mary involved now?" Roxanne was rapidly losing her patience with her husband.

Before Tim had a chance to answer her, she noticed that they had an audience. Several people were sitting outside at a nearby coffee house, watching them fight. She recognized many of the faces and shook her head.

"Oh, that's just great!" Roxanne exclaimed, as she pointed her thumb in the direction of the gawkers. "Now we get to be the talk of the town."

With that, she stormed up the street, leaving Tim behind. He had no desire to go after her again. Tim turned around and headed in the opposite direction, toward the nearest pub.

When Tim walked into the inn about three hours later, Roxanne was waiting for him in the lobby. They didn't currently have any guests, due to the earthquake devastation of the island, so she just sat on the lobby couch, reading a book, until he got home. She knew he couldn't go far. They were on an island after all. When he started pounding on the front door, Roxanne jumped up to unlock it.

"Hi Baby Doll." Tim slurred his words.

"You're drunk."

"Well you got that right!" he told her, laughing.

"What are you wearing?" Roxanne asked him, looking at the baggy denim overalls he had on. He did not own a pair of overalls.

"What? Oh these?" Tim slurred out as he tugged on one of the straps. "Dooley was at the pub and gave me to them to wear. I mean gave me to them to wear. I mean, whatever. You know what I mean."

Roxanne couldn't help but chuckle at his inability to form a coherent sentence.

"Yeah, I know what you mean. It's time for bed."

She struggled to help him up the stairs to the top floor where they lived. Tim was making a lot of noise, despite her best efforts to keep him quiet. She put him to bed in their room so she could keep a close eye on him, even though he had been sleeping in another room. Roxanne knew that she was going to have to explain something to the girls in the morning. If she was lucky, maybe they would sleep through it. Kids could be really deep sleepers.

The next morning, Piper was combing the wet tangles out of her long blonde hair, when a message popped up on her computer screen.

Piper walked over to see who it was, expecting to see something from one of her friends. She was wrong.

'I'm back,' Anonymous typed.

"Oh my god," Piper exclaimed out loud, though she was completely alone in her bedroom.

She ran out her bedroom door, to Mary's room next door and knocked. Without waiting for an answer, Piper opened the door and walked in. Mary was still asleep.

"Mary," Piper whispered, not wanting to startle her sister. But she got no response.

Piper nudged Mary's left shoulder, hoping that would work. She didn't want to talk too loudly, afraid that she might wake up her parents.

"Whaaat?" Mary dragged out her question in a mumbly, half asleep, sort of way.

"Get up, I need to talk to you. It's important," Piper ordered.

"I'm trying to sleep. Do you mind?" Mary rolled over onto her left side, away from Piper.

"I'm not kidding. You need to get up!" Piper said louder than she meant to, as she grabbed the blankets off of Mary and threw them to the foot of the bed.

"Piper, what?" Mary said with a frown as she sat up and stretched her arms high over her head.

"I got another message on the computer. You need to come to my room. Now," Piper ordered her.

"Oh, okay fine. I'm coming." Mary grabbed her lavender robe and matching slippers and followed Piper to her room.

As they sat down, they saw that there was another message on the computer.

'You there?' it said.

"Should I answer?" Piper asked Mary.

"Yes, answer him." Mary rubbed the sleep from her eyes and tried to smooth out the tangled blonde hair that was sticking up everywhere.

'Yes, I'm here. What do you want?' Piper typed.

'$10,000.'

Piper and Mary looked at each other.

"Is he kidding? Where does he think we can get that kind of money? He knows we are only 15 years old, right?" Mary asked.

"I'm sure he does. He figured out how to send these messages to us, so he obviously knows who we are," Piper replied. "What should I say back?"

"Here, move over," Mary replied, pushing her sister a bit to the side and turning the laptop computer toward herself.

'Why would we give you $10,000 when we've already told the sheriff what happened on the beach?' Mary typed in.

'The sheriff doesn't know everything. Does he?'

"What does that mean?" Piper asked her sister.

'Yes, we told him everything,' Mary typed back.

'I don't think you did. I have a video that no one has seen.'

"Holy crap. Do you think he's telling us the truth?" Piper asked Mary.

Mary shrugged her shoulders.

'What's on the video?' Mary replied to Anonymous.

'It shows someone you know, with a drunk Alex. I'll leave the rest to your imagination. So, do you wanna know which one of your friends killed Alex?'

'Yes. Who killed him?' Mary typed.

'Get that $10,000 to me and you can see the video for yourself.'

'We don't have that kind of money,' Mary replied.

'Figure it out. I know one of your group has wealthy parents.' With that, Anonymous logged off.

"Who is he talking about?" Mary asked Piper. "Who has wealthy parents?"

Piper thought for a moment. "He must be talking about Dixie. She is the only one I know that has a lot of money."

"What are we going to do now?" Mary asked.

"I have no idea. I know I didn't kill Alex, but obviously someone did. I don't know why I'm the one getting harassed. None of the other girls have said anything about anyone making this kind of contact with them," Piper told her.

"Girls, it's time for breakfast!" Roxanne yelled up the stairs.

The family tried to get together for breakfast outside at the cafe as often as possible. The twins sat quietly, deep in thought, while eating their blueberry waffles. Neither one had noticed the noise their parents made the night before, when Roxanne was trying to get an intoxicated Tim up the stairs. Roxanne was still a bit irritated with Tim, but mostly over it by the time they sat down for the family meal. Tim had a dull headache, punctuated by a queasy stomach, and only ate a piece of dry toast with milk. It was all his poor body could take that morning. His daughters, having other things on their minds, didn't seem to notice anything was amiss.

CHAPTER 18

"Hey, Cecily." Piper stopped in on her way to work. "I need to talk to you. Do you have a few minutes?"

"Sure, Sweetheart. Anything for you. Do we need to worry about prying ears?" Cecily lowered her voice and looked around.

"Yes." Piper also lowered her voice.

With their heads together, anyone watching them would have thought they were up to something.

"Okay. You grab a blanket, I'll grab us some sodas and meet you back here in five minutes," Cecily ordered.

As they walked down to the beach a few minutes later, neither one said a word. When they found the perfect spot, far away from prying ears, Piper spread out the blanket and they both sat down, cross legged. Cecily handed a cherry soda can to Piper.

"So, what do you want to talk about?" Cecily asked her.

Piper took a deep breath. She knew Cecily could be trusted, but it made her nervous anyway. Too many people knowing what was going on could be a problem. Secrets were not well kept on a small island such as theirs.

"Mary and I were on the computer and someone messaged us. We don't know who," Piper told her.

"What did the message say?" Cecily whispered, her curiosity piqued.

"Why are you whispering?" Piper asked her.

"I don't know," Cecily looked around. "It just seems like the thing to do."

"Well anyway, the messages just said that he knows our secret."

"Are there any clues on there about who he might be?" Cecily asked her.

"No, nothing. But I think someone must have been at the Cove that day. Someone we didn't see. Who else?"

"I don't know. We'll have to see if we can figure it out. Does anyone else, besides you four girls and me, know about that day?" Cecily asked her.

"Mary knows. My parents know. Plus I know Dixie has told some people. So, it's not a complete secret. Oh, and the sheriff knows too. So, I guess a lot of people know. But, they only know that we found Alex like that. This person messaging us kind of makes it sound like they know more. Like they were there when the beating took place. It is possible that someone could have been hiding over by the cliffs," Piper explained.

"Yeah, it's possible, I guess," Cecily replied. "It sounds like half the island knows by now. So someone must have photos or video. Otherwise, why would they think they can hold this over you?"

"Yeah, that's true. He said he has a video," Piper lamented. "Oh wait, there's one more thing. He wants $10,000."

"What?! Why didn't you lead with that? Holy cow."

Piper shrugged. "I just remembered."

Piper didn't seem to Cecily that she was taking the whole thing all that seriously. How in the world could she forget $10,000? Cecily thought.

"Why would he think you have that kind of money?"

"I guess he thinks we can get it from Dixie. Well her father anyway. We definitely don't have it. My parents put all of their money back into the business, especially now that the wave has hurt things big time," Piper told her.

"We need to get to the bottom of this. I have an idea. Bring your computer to the bar. We do know someone that is a computer whiz. She can probably figure out who's behind this," Cecily said.

"Okay. I have a couple things to do. Meet in about an hour?" Piper asked her.

"Perfect."

An hour later, Piper walked into the Wildflower bar with her laptop computer and set it down on the bar top. The bar had not opened yet. Cecily was there getting it ready, checking the inventory, and gossiping with a couple of inn guests that had wandered through the bar.

"You aren't telling anyone about my 'thing,' are you?" Piper asked her, as she looked over at the couple standing at the end of the bar.

"We'll see you later, got some sightseeing to do." The couple waved to Cecily as they walked out the door.

Cecily smiled back at them and waited until they were completely out the door before she responded to Piper.

"I told you I would keep my big mouth shut, and I will. I promise." Cecily gave her a serious look.

"Okay, sorry. This is a small island, you know?"

"I know."

Right then, Anna walked through the bar, waving hi as she walked by.

"Hey miss Wildflower! Just the person I need. I've been looking for you," Cecily stopped her.

"Me? Why?" Anna scrunched her face up.

"We need your computer expertise," Cecily told her.

"Really? For what? You know I'm not really allowed to use the computer."

"I know. But, I also know that you do work for Roxanne on her computer. So, you don't seem all that worried about it," Cecily replied.

Anna thought a moment about what Cecily just said. She wasn't wrong. "Well, okay. What do you need?" Anna relented.

Turning to Piper, "I guess I should make sure it is all right with you that we get Anna involved. I mean she is going to find out if she starts digging around on your computer. Is it okay with you?" Cecily asked her.

Piper looked over at Anna and back to Cecily, feeling really put on the spot. How could she say no without looking like a complete jerk?

Right then, Mary walked in and was surprised to see Cecily, Piper, and Anna standing around talking. It wasn't a group that usually hung out together.

"Hi," she said to all three of them, with a questioning look on her face.

"Hi Mary," they replied.

"Um, Cecily, I can't find my mom. Can you tell her I went for a walk on the beach and will be back in a while?"

"Sure. Don't be gone too long. You know how she worries about you."

"I won't." Mary walked out the door.

Once she was gone, the topic in the bar turned back to what they wanted from Anna.

"Yeah, I guess it's fine if Anna knows." Piper responded to the question that was left hanging in the air when Mary walked in. "But, Anna you need to make sure you don't tell anyone," Piper said to her.

"Um, okay. What do you need?"

Cecily proceeded to explain to Anna exactly what they were after. They showed her the instant messages and asked her if she could figure out who sent them.

"Yeah, that would be pretty easy," Anna told her. Then turning to Piper, "Do you know who killed Alex?"

Piper was surprised that Anna would be so brazen as to directly ask her that question. She was hoping that Anna could find out the problem without actually needing to know the dirty details.

"Hey, don't worry about that," Cecily jumped in. "We just need you to figure this out. Will you help us?"

"Okay sure. But, if I get into trouble for this, I'm naming names," Anna said seriously.

"Fair enough," Cecily replied.

"Piper, leave your computer with me, I'll take it up to my room, so no one knows what I'm doing. Give me a couple of days, okay?"

"Sure, that's fine. Thank you very much," Piper replied, hugging Anna. "I'm sorry that we can't tell you much. It's kind of private, and really serious, you know?"

"Yeah, it's definitely serious." Anna closed the laptop and tucked it under her left arm, as she headed upstairs to stash it in her room. She shared a room with Frankie and wanted to make sure it was hidden well.

"Thanks for this," Piper told Cecily after Anna left. "I didn't even think of asking Anna for help. I gotta go do some stuff. See you later."

Piper walked out the door to find Mary and found her sitting at one of the tables of the outdoor cafe reading. She plopped herself down in a chair opposite of her sister. Mary looked up very briefly and went back to her book without acknowledging Piper's presence.

"Hey, I thought you were going for a walk on the beach."

"I changed my mind. What do you want?" Mary wanted to be left alone to read, something she didn't have a chance to do as much as she would like.

"Mary, I need to talk to you."

Mary didn't even look up from her book. "About what?"

"I need to go somewhere to do something and I need you to cover for me."

"Well that clears things up. Why do I need to cover for you?" Mary asked.

"Because I don't want Mom and Dad to know. They'll be really mad. I'll tell them I'm walking on the beach, but I'm going to go check something out. If they come looking for me, pretend like you're me, okay? You've done it a million times."

Mary continued reading, completely ignoring her sister.

"Mary! Will you or won't you?" Piper asked her again.

Mary jumped then, startled back to reality, and was clearly

annoyed at the interruption. She didn't care what Piper was up to. She just wanted her sister to leave her alone.

"Fine, whatever," Mary replied, not missing a beat in her book.

"You are gonna have to go change first," Piper said, looking at Mary from head to toe. She was wearing a long, loose dress that brushed her ankles and had on a beaded necklace that she made herself.

"No, I don't want to."

"Pleeeeease, Mary. This is really important," Piper begged. "Mom and Dad will never think you are me in that getup."

Mary slammed her book down on the table and stood up. "It's not a 'getup.' This better be important."

She headed up to the top floor of the inn. When Mary returned five minutes later, she had on shorts, a t-shirt, and sneakers. Her outfit was almost identical to Pipers.

"Are those my clothes?" Piper asked her.

"Yes, what about it?" Mary sat down and picked up her book again.

"Nothing." Piper would normally throw a fit if Mary wore her clothes. It was one of the main things they fought about. She didn't dare say anything this time.

Piper jumped onto her bicycle and headed down the street. Mary never even looked up.

"Piper!" Mary heard her father calling her sister. She was still sitting outside, engrossed in her novel.

Oh shoot, Mary thought to herself. She knew Piper wasn't back from wherever she went and she had kind of promised her sister that she would help her not get into trouble for being gone. It was time for her to kick her acting into high gear.

"What, Daddy?" Mary asked when Tim walked out onto the deck of the cafe.

Mary was pretty good at pretending to be Piper. She had done it many times over the years when Piper was doing something she shouldn't have been doing. Even as far back as 5 years old, Mary could always fool her father. Her mother was a different story. She frequently saw through the ruse, but not always. It was a bit of a crap shoot with their mother.

"Piper, where have you been? I've been looking everywhere for you," Tim asked Mary.

"Just outside, walking on the beach," Mary replied. "Now I'm reading."

"Where's your sister?"

"I think she's up in her room. She said she wasn't feeling well, so she's taking a nap."

"Oh, okay. Can you help me work here at the cafe? It's starting to get pretty busy and it's too much for Frankie alone."

Mary looked around her. She was so caught up in her novel that she hadn't even noticed all the people around her. They were chattering on and it was quite noisy. She was surprised that she had been oblivious to it all.

"Okay."

Mary walked over, picked up a bucket, and started clearing tables. She had been there about a half hour when her mother walked in.

"Mary, where's your sister?" Roxanne asked her, looking at her clothing. It was unusual for Mary to be dressed the way she was.

"Um, I'm Piper. Mary's upstairs."

Roxanne eyed her daughter suspiciously. When Mary twisted her hair, a nervous habit she had acquired over the years, Roxanne knew she was lying. It was something she had never seen Piper do.

"Really?" Roxanne confronted her.

"Yeah." Mary turned around quickly and started clearing off the table that a family of five had just vacated, hoping her mother would take her word for it and leave.

"Whoa, hold on a minute young lady. Come here." Roxanne was not buying the act.

Mary put the plates back down on the table and dutifully walked back to her mother.

"Follow me." Roxanne turned and walked into the inn. There was a door that led directly from the outdoor cafe into the lobby of the inn.

"Sit." Roxanne pointed at the couch.

Mary sat.

"Take off your left shoe."

"What? Why?" Mary didn't know what her left shoe had to do with anything.

"Just do it."

As Mary complied with her mother's demand, it dawned on her where her mother was heading when she told her to remove her shoe.

"Yeah, that's what I thought," Roxanne said, looking at Mary's left foot. It was the foot that she got the three inch scar on the day the teenagers took her and Piper to Edgewater Rock and dragged them off the cliff.

Mary could not have possibly looked more guilty.

"Where is she, Mary?"

Mary looked down at her feet, ashamed at her attempt to impersonate her sister.

"I don't know, really," she said as she put her shoe back on. "She just said she had something to do and needed me to cover for her." Mary couldn't look her mother in the eyes.

"Go up to your room. I'll deal with you later."

About an hour later, Piper walked in. Both of her parents were standing by the front door with worry on their faces. Piper knew immediately that the jig was up.

"Where have you been?" Tim asked her.

She couldn't think of a good lie right on the spot. "I, um, went over to Dixie's house. To look around." She told the truth.

"What do you mean 'to look around'? You can't just go look around people's houses. And, why would you?" Roxanne was quite unhappy with her daughter's answer.

"I didn't go in her house. I just looked around the yard. There's gotta be some reason why people think Dixie killed Alex. I didn't go in, I swear. But, I knew that Dixie's parents were out of town, so I just went to look around when I knew she wasn't at home."

Piper had no intention of telling her parents that she actually did go into Dixie's house. They never locked their doors. Hardly anyone in town did. She didn't find anything helpful in the house. She had concentrated mostly on Dixie's room. Nothing.

"Does Dixie know you were there?"

"No. I left before she got back. I'm sorry."

"Go up to your room. We'll talk later." Roxanne pointed toward the stairs. Piper left without another word.

CHAPTER 19

"Hey, Frankie!" She heard his voice calling her from the entrance to the cafe behind her and she smiled without realizing it.

Frankie turned around and ran across the cafe, every patron watching her, as she jumped into Sawyer's arms, her red hair flailing about. Every single customer at the cafe smiled at their reunion, happy for the reunited couple. Most of them averted their eyes when Frankie and Sawyer started kissing, which was a bit much for an afternoon at the cafe. For a few minutes, she completely forgot her obligation to her customers. Food was left unserved. Glasses were left unfilled. Her customers knew the story and they didn't mind. Frankie was a favorite of all the locals that frequented the cafe, those that didn't think she was guilty of murder, that is. Actually Sawyer was also very well liked. Sure, some people thought she was involved in killing Alex. Most did not.

After giving them a few minutes together, a few of her customers got up and congratulated Sawyer on being released from jail. They wished them good luck with everything, on their way out of the cafe. Though she neglected all of them once Sawyer showed up, almost everyone left her a generous tip. It was a good day for Frankie.

"Frankie," she heard Roxanne say sternly.

It jerked Frankie back to reality as she pulled away from Sawyer's loving arms.

"Oh, Roxanne, I'm sorry. I'll get everything done right away."

Frankie kissed Sawyer quickly one last time and sent him on his way, with a promise that they would meet up after her shift was over. Roxanne watched her work for a few minutes, before returning back inside the inn to get some of her own work done.

"How did you get out?" Frankie asked Sawyer later that afternoon as they walked hand in hand along the beach.

"The sheriff said they didn't have enough evidence against me, and that having an argument with Alex that day wasn't enough to hold me. So, here I am."

He smiled that incredibly cute smile that Frankie had come to love. Stopping to face him, she smiled back, looking into his big brown eyes, as she reached up and ran her fingers through his wavy, sandy blond hair. A seagull squawked as it flew overhead and they both looked up, laughing.

"Sawyer?"

"Yes," he replied, caressing her left cheek, ever so gently.

"I need to tell you something."

"What is it, Sweetheart?"

Frankie stepped back away from him and burst out crying, covering her face with her hands. Sawyer stepped closer and and wrapped his arms around her.

"What's the matter?" he asked her.

"It's my fault you were in prison."

"Jail, Frankie. It was just a holding cell at the sheriff's office. Definitely not prison." He smiled, wondering if she had been picturing him in a maximum security prison, sharing a cell with a guy named Big Bertha. He burst out laughing.

"Don't laugh at me." Frankie was embarrassed and slapped him on the arm.

"Oh, Sweetheart, I'm sorry. I promise I'm not laughing at you. I was just thinking about what prison would be like."

"And that made you laugh?" Her eyes widened with surprise.

"Well, yeah. It's not really funny, I guess, now that I think about it. Thank god I wasn't in prison. Anyway, what did you want to tell me? Why do you think it's your fault that I was in jail?" he asked her as he removed himself from the bear hug he had on her.

Frankie spent the next several minutes telling him why it was her fault that he was in jail. Sawyer stood there, silently, letting her speak, the frown on his face deepening by the minute. When she was done speaking, he looked away, deep in thought. His eyes seemed shaded by a hundred unspoken opinions. She reached for his hands in a comforting gesture.

"How the hell could you do that?!" he yelled at her as he jerked his hands away from her. "I don't know you at all!"

"I'm sorry," Frankie wailed. "It was just on the spur of the moment. It was stupid, I know. Really stupid. Now you are getting blamed for Alex's death when it wasn't your fault. It's my fault you went to jail. I'm really, really sorry."

"You're sorry?! Are you kidding me? You do that and then let the sheriff arrest me? I spent several days in jail for something I didn't do!"

Sawyer was furious. He glared at Frankie and stormed away. When he looked back, she was following him, which made him stop and turn to face her.

"Don't you dare follow me. I want nothing to do with you right now. Just leave me alone!"

Frankie just stood there sobbing on the beach as Sawyer took off running. It seemed to her that he couldn't get away from her fast enough. She knew that it would take a long time, if ever, before he could forgive her. After a few minutes, she composed herself enough to walk back up to the Wildflower Inn. She just wanted to go to her room and crawl in bed forever. She knew that wasn't going to happen though. After what she told Sawyer, she completely expected the sheriff to show up at any moment looking for her.

As she walked up the wooden steps to the outdoor cafe, Piper caught up to her and informed her that the girls were all having a meeting at the lighthouse in an hour. Frankie told her she would be there.

Built in the 1800s to aid the mariners in dangerous, rocky waters, the Wildflower Island Lighthouse had been damaged several times over the centuries by massive storms. It had been patched and refurbished dozens of times. This particular lighthouse was originally built using stone, and the keeper's house stood next to it. There is an outside entrance to the lighthouse, as well as one from the keeper's house, long since abandoned and boarded up.

There once was a bright light that shone far out into the sea, to aid mariners in navigation. It no longer operated, as modern ship navigation took over, rendering the lighthouse obsolete. The operation of the lighthouse was retired altogether in the 1970s.

When Piper and Frankie arrived at the lighthouse a bit more than an hour later, they could see that the other two girls were already there. Or at least someone was. From the outside, they could see bits of light bouncing around off the walls and out of the windows, into the night. Ivy clung to the worn stone walls and rattled in the breeze. A dog barked off in the distance as Piper opened the squeaky door leading inside. Frankie followed her in.

Piper and Mary had spent many fun times over the years in the top of the lighthouse. They would bring blankets and snacks and hang out for hours, watching the ocean. Tim and Roxanne knew exactly where they were and said it was fine. Tim had fond memories of his time as a kid playing in the lighthouse with his friends.

As Piper and Frankie ascended the steep, winding, metal stairs, they hung on tightly to the railing.

"Are you guys up there?!" Piper yelled from about one third of the way up.

"Yeah, it's us!" Olivia yelled back.

"Why did you yell up? We saw the lights when we walked up," Frankie asked her, as she breathed deeply, trying to catch her breath. It was a steep climb.

"Just making sure," Piper replied, taking in deep breaths herself. "I don't know what kind of crazies might be hanging out up there," she replied, looking up.

The local kids didn't seem to use the lighthouse much anymore. Piper noticed a layer of dust, some of it recently disturbed by the two girls that arrived ahead of them. The staircase was once wooden, long ago, but at one point the wooden stairs were replaced with wrought iron. The staircase railings had many spots of rust that the girls tried to avoid, not wanting to cut their hands on it. Frankie looked out one of the dirty windows they passed on their way up, hoping to catch a glimpse of Sawyer. He wasn't anywhere around though, not that she really expected him to be.

"It's about time," Dixie exclaimed as they rounded the final curve and stepped onto the landing at the top. "It's mega creepy up here."

"Sorry. We got here as fast as we could," Piper replied.

Piper was the only one that had thought to bring a blanket. She spread it out on the metal landing and they all sat down in a circle of sorts.

"I need to talk to you about that person that messaged me the other day," Piper started. "He sent me another message."

"Oh no," Dixie responded. "What did he say?" She covered her mouth with her left hand, fear showing in her eyes. Her gold bracelets clanging together, making quite a racket as they echoed off the stone walls.

"Seriously Dixie? Those bracelets again?" Olivia asked, with a pinched look on her face.

Dixie looked down at her wrist. "Oh sorry. I guess they are kinda loud in here." She pulled them off her wrist and laid them down on the metal landing next to her.

"There were a couple of things, actually. First, he said he has a video of someone with Alex at the Cove. He said it was someone I know, said it was one of my friends," Piper told them.

"Who did he say it was?" Frankie asked, a bit too fast, as far as Piper was concerned. Piper studied Frankie's face for a moment.

"He didn't. That's where the next thing comes in. He wants $10,000 to give us the video. Or show it to us at least," Piper told them.

"What? Where in the world does he think we can get $10,000?" Olivia asked.

"He said that he knows one of us has wealthy parents." When Piper told them that, every girl turned to look at Dixie.

"What?" Dixie asked, as she looked into the eyes of each girl. "Me? No, I could never get that kind of money."

"Isn't your dad a rich attorney?" Frankie asked her. "I haven't lived here that long and even I know that. And you live in that huge stone house up on the hill, right?"

"Well, um, yes," Dixie replied. "But it's not my money. My dad will never give me that much. Not in a million years. Your parents own the Wildflower Inn and Cafe, Piper. So, what about you?"

Everyone turned toward Piper.

"What about me? I don't have that kind of money. Not even close. Besides, let the blackmailer show his video to the cops. I don't care. I know I didn't do anything wrong," Piper stated adamantly.

"So, unless one of you did it," Piper said with a chuckle, "then I say ignore this guy. His video can't hurt any of us. He said it was one of my friends, but really, that could be anyone we go to school with."

"But what if it is one of us?" Frankie asked.

Each girl looked around at the others suspiciously. None of them responding immediately.

"Well I know for a fact it wasn't me," Piper answered. "And, since Olivia was with me, it wasn't her either. That's all I know for sure."

"Are we seriously going to have this argument again?" Dixie asked. "We are getting nowhere. I really don't think it was any of the four of us. But, we need to figure out who it was. We need to get to the bottom of this. Now even Alex's dad is accusing me. My guts are always in a knot and I'm tired of it."

"Yeah, I agree," Piper chimed in. "Now, Frankie," she said as she turned to speak to Frankie directly, "I know you aren't going to like this, but it might be a good idea for you to stop seeing Sawyer. For now anyway. I've heard people around town say that they think you are involved in this, but no one thinks Sawyer is. Sawyer is a nice guy. I don't want him getting into anymore trouble because of you. Being with you makes him look bad. Do you want that?" Piper did her best to sound worried about Frankie and Sawyer.

"She has a point," Olivia added.

"Yeah, that's not gonna be a problem," Frankie told them. "He dumped me."

"What? Why?" Dixie asked. "I thought you two were in looove?" Dixie made smooching noises as she drawled out the word 'love.'

Frankie hesitated just a bit longer than she should, which made the girls a bit nervous, wondering what happened.

"I would rather not say. It's personal. My presence shouldn't hurt Sawyer anymore." Frankie looked down into her lap, not wanting to make anymore eye contact with her cohorts.

"Does he know something that we should know?" Olivia asked her, as she watched Frankie's mannerisms closely.

Frankie did seem a bit twitchy to Olivia. The other girls noticed it too. No one said it out loud for fear of repercussions, but they all suspected Frankie was involved somehow. None of them were sure she actually wielded the deadly rock, but they felt she was involved. They just didn't know how. Not yet anyway.

"No! I said it's personal. That means it is none of your business!"

Frankie jumped up. She was done with the whole thing and just wanted to get out of there. Just as she started down the first steep step, someone opened the door below. It was rusty, and the heavy metal frame of the door made a high pitched squeaking noise under the pressure of someone opening it, ever so slowly. Frankie carefully backed up to where the girls were sitting. She sat back down and they all moved a little closer to each other, for comfort mostly, none of them daring to make a peep.

CHAPTER 20

"Are you guys up there?" came a loud whisper from below. "It's me, Mary."

The four sitting girls stood up then, relief flooding their faces.

"Yes, it's us!" Piper yelled down the stairs, as she leaned over to get a look at Mary on the bottom landing.

Mary raced to the top as they stood waiting.

"What are you doing here?" Dixie asked her as Mary rounded the last few steps.

Mary was breathing quite heavily and bent over to catch her breath.

"Hold…wait…hold on. I…can't…breathe," Mary managed to say between rapid breaths.

After a full minute, she was composed enough to speak.

"Oh my god. Whew. I ran the entire way here, then up those damn stairs. I need to get into better shape," Mary told them, her breathing almost back to normal.

The four girls stood watching her, as they waited for her to state her purpose in running all the way over. Something was obviously urgent.

"I came to tell you all that the sheriff is looking for you," Mary told them. "Well actually Dixie, I think."

"What? Me? Why?" Dixie looked worried, as she nervously tugged at the long abalone earrings she was sporting. She had recently purchased them at one of the local gift shops and thought that the shiny blue and green earrings were just beautiful.

"I don't really know. He came to the inn to ask my mom and dad if they had seen you. He said he's been looking all over for you," Mary answered. "My mom told him that Piper was here with friends and you might be with them."

"Oh my god. I need to get out of here. Dealing with the sheriff right now is the last thing I need. I better go see my dad and let him help."

Dixie started down the stairs, while the four girls followed her slow descent. Because the stairs were very steep and winding, it was foolish for anyone to try to get to the bottom quickly. One misstep could be deadly. When they reached the bottom and walked out the door, the sheriff was parked outside. He was leaning on his closed truck door with his arms folded. It was pretty obvious that he had been waiting for them.

"Oh, hi Sheriff," Mary said first.

"Mary," he said and nodded his head. "You sure can run fast. You on the track team at school?"

"No sir." Mary tried not to look directly at the sheriff. She felt very guilty for running over and warning them of his impending arrival.

Mary knew she had been caught. Apparently running out of the inn right after her mother told the sheriff that Piper was at the lighthouse, didn't fool him a bit. He probably jumped into his truck within minutes and drove straight over. Of course Mary had cut through the streets and down the beach, which was a shorter way, as the crow flies, they say. So it took the sheriff a couple more minutes by truck.

"Miss Bradford, I would like to speak with you. In private," he said to Dixie. "The rest of you girls can wait over there. Don't go anywhere," he warned them, as he nodded his head in the direction of the beach.

"Okay Sheriff. Should I call my dad?" Dixie asked him.

Rex knew Mitchell Bradford well. They had many legal dealings over the years. Some of the cases they worked on the same side, most of them not. Mitchell Bradford was a defense attorney, so he and Rex weren't on the same side often. It was Rex's job to catch the bad guy. It was Mitchell's job to get him acquitted. The best anyone could say about them was that the two men tolerated one another.

"I don't know. Should you?"

"What is that supposed to mean?" Dixie asked, pulling on her earrings again.

Rex decided that playing the aggressive sheriff was probably not the way to go with this young girl. He needed to be careful how he talked to her and with what he asked her. He did not want to get a phone call from her father when she arrived home later.

"Look, I just want to talk to you for a minute. Can we do that?" Rex asked her. "Let's walk," he said, as he started walking up the path, toward the road. Dixie followed him.

"Sure, that's fine, I guess," she replied, as she caught up and started walking beside him.

"Oh, is this yours?" Rex asked her casually, as he pulled something shiny from his uniform pants pocket.

"Oh yeah, where did you find it?" Dixie replied, as she reached for her broken bracelet. "It broke the other day and…oh."

Dixie immediately stopped speaking in the middle of her sentence as the realization hit her. Rex watched her reaction carefully as he pulled the bracelet back out of her reach. It was evidence in a murder investigation.

"Do you know where the bracelet turned up?" he asked her.

Dixie was looking at her own feet intently. She dared not look up into his face.

"Um, I, um, no. I don't remember where I lost it."

"Perhaps you were with Alex Spencer when it broke? Does that sound about right? We found it on his body."

Dixie knew she was busted. She knew that the sheriff suspected her.

Otherwise he would not be showing the bracelet to her now. The coroner had found her bracelet in Alex's pocket. She saw him that day. That fateful day. And they had fought. She was angry with him for whatever it was he had with Frankie. She claimed he was stalking her. He claimed that he and Frankie were seeing each other. Dixie didn't know what to think. Either way, she didn't like it. Yes, she dated other guys, but it didn't matter. He belonged to her and she let him know it that day.

The two of them had a big blowup about it and she had swung at him, in a feeble attempt to slap him across the face. He was quicker than she was and grabbed her wrist right before contact was made with his face, breaking her bracelet. Neither one of them noticed, as they were so focused on that slap, or attempted slap. He told her they were through. He wanted nothing more to do with her. He wanted someone else and that was all that mattered to him.

Later, when Dixie realized her bracelet was missing, she figured she had probably lost it when she and Alex fought. She knew she would probably never find it in the sand, in the middle of the beach, so she just let it go. It never dawned on her that Alex would pick it up and put it in his pocket.

Against her better judgment, because she had been taught many times over the years to never talk to law enforcement without her father present, Dixie explained her fight with Alex. She told him that Alex was drunk and how they got into an argument. Then she tried to slap him and how he grabbed her arm and must have broken the bracelet then. She said she didn't even realized that it happened, but he must have picked it up and put it in his pocket after she stormed off.

"So, let me see if I got this right. You had a fight with Alex about Frankie. Then when he tried to stop you from slapping him, your bracelet broke, and you just walked away. Is that your story? Are you leaving anything out? Like how you maybe picked up a rock and bashed him over the head?"

Dixie gasped. She wasn't stupid and knew that the sheriff was trying to rule people out, but until that moment she hadn't realized that she might actually be a suspect. Not much scared her, but the sheriff succeeded in scaring her then.

"No Sheriff. I swear. It's not a story. I was pissed off at him, sure. But, I would never kill him." Dixie paused for just a moment. "I think I need to call my dad now."

"Yeah, that's probably a good idea," Rex agreed.

By 8:00 a.m. the next morning, it was all over town. The gossip spread like wildfire, even surpassing the speed of Cecily. Everyone knew that Dixie was in big trouble. She hadn't been arrested. Not yet, anyway. But, if you listened to anyone in town, it was coming soon.

Dixie had been spotted in the back of the sheriff's truck between the lighthouse and the station. The other four girls walked home after the sheriff talked to them a bit. They really couldn't add anything to what Rex already knew, so he told them to go home and he would talk to them later. The girls scattered, each heading toward her own home. Piper and Mary walked together, mostly in silence, neither one of them bringing up Dixie.

Mitchell Bradford arrived at the sheriff's station shortly after Rex and Dixie arrived. His daughter was sitting in a chair in the outer office, drinking hot chocolate when he got there. Ten minutes later, the two of them walked out the door.

Sheriff Rex told Mitchell exactly why he had picked up Dixie and that he was not arresting her. Not just yet. He just wanted to talk to them. But, he would be investigating the matter very thoroughly. Mitchell and Rex could be heard arguing all through the building and the employees listened with great interest. They all watched Dixie's reaction to the ruckus, but no one spoke to her, per the sheriff's orders. She was a minor and he didn't want any trouble from her attorney father.

After several minutes, Mitchell stormed out of Rex's office, slammed the door behind him, and took hold of his daughter's arm.

"Let's go. We are done here," he told Dixie, as he dragged her out of the office.

He turned back to glare at Rex, and saw Rex watching him and his daughter through the glass office walls. Mitchell slammed the outer building door as they left.

The next day, Dixie walked over to the Wildflower Inn to talk to Frankie. Along the way, she received many glaring looks from the locals. She tried her best to ignore them, but it wasn't easy. She found herself yelling at them to leave her alone, something she knew she shouldn't do. It wasn't going to solve or even help anything, but she couldn't help herself. Her father had given her permission to go to the inn, under strict orders not to talk to anyone about the case. She agreed.

She had nothing to add to the growing suspicion against her. Against her father's orders, she told anyone that would listen that she didn't do it. She didn't know who did, but it wasn't her. No one believed her. Everyone had already heard the story of how she was seeing Alex Spencer and that she got extremely jealous, going into a rage and bashing his head in with a rock. Each time the story was repeated, it got worse. By the time some people heard it, she was there with a bunch of thugs and they all ganged up on poor Alex and killed him viciously.

No one, except Frankie, would have anything to do with Dixie. Frankie talked to her some, but even she wanted to be distanced from Dixie. Guilty or not, Frankie didn't want to be associated with her. She was terrified that the stories of Dixie killing Alex would start including her name. There were already several people in town that thought Frankie might have done it.

"Hi Piper," Dixie said to her as Piper walked out to the cafe.

Piper stopped, surprise showing in her eyes as she looked at Dixie and Frankie sitting at one of the tables. "Oh Dixie, I don't think you should be here. My parents would not be happy about it," Piper told her, trying to be gentle.

"Why? I didn't do anything."

"Maybe you did, maybe you didn't. But, everybody in town thinks you did. Or most everybody anyway. It's all the town is talking about," Piper replied.

Just then, a middle aged couple that Piper knew from them eating at the cafe often, walked up the steps, looked over at the three girls, settling on Dixie. Then they looked at each other, turned around and left, without saying a word.

"See," Piper said, as she pointed at the couple. "That's what I mean. We are losing business already. You really have to go. I'm sorry."

Dixie got it, though she was miffed at Piper for being so harsh. Piper could have been kinder as she kicked Dixie to the curb.

"Fine, I'm going," Dixie said angrily as she waved her hand at Piper in a dismissive way. "I don't want to stay where I'm not wanted."

With that, Dixie stood up and stormed off the cafe deck toward home.

"You didn't have to do that," Frankie said to Piper.

"Yes I did. Look, I don't know if Dixie killed Alex or not, but many people obviously think she did. And this is my parents' business. With her here, we are losing money, and we can't afford to do that. You have to understand." Piper tried to explain her actions to Frankie.

"Well I don't. You can't go around treating people like that. Especially when it's just a rumor," Frankie argued.

"You just don't get it," Piper said as she turned and left in a huff.

CHAPTER 21

Javier Lopez was the town celebrity. He was a movie star and the island's claim to fame. He grew up in the town of Sea Cove and knew pretty much everyone in town. Now in his 20s they just treated him like every other local. The locals nodded when they saw him on the street or waved as they passed by. That's how everyone was treated. No one really cared that he was famous. He was just Javier, the fat little kid that used to go into the ice cream store and sit at the counter for hours during his summer vacation.

No longer the fat little kid, Javier was tall, thin, and gorgeous, even by Hollywood's standards. He was also one of the biggest movie stars in the world. Still, he was just another local in Sea Cove. Occasionally a tourist would spot him walking down the street and the chase was on. Javier got really good at ducking into the local shops and disappearing. The shop owners all knew his predicament well, and were happy to let him run into the back room, out of sight, until his fans gave up looking for him.

"Oh my god, is that Javier Lopez?" Cecily's college roommate asked her as they were eating lunch outside one of the outdoor cafes that lined the main street of Sea Cove.

Cecily looked in the direction her friend, Jennifer, was pointing.

"Yeah, that's him," turning back to Jennifer. "So, what were you saying about your parents?" Cecily tried to change the subject. Javier's fans could be extremely annoying.

"Do you think he'll give me his autograph? My friends would freak!" Jennifer exclaimed.

Knowing that her friend would probably be distracted for the rest of their lunch together, Cecily decided to deal with it and hopefully they could get back to their nice lunch.

"I don't know. Let's find out. Hey Jav, come over here!" Cecily yelled to where he was standing across the street.

"What the…you know Javier Lopez?" Her friend's eyes became very wide.

"Yes. We grew up together. He's my best friend."

"Hey Cec, what's up?" Javier said as he walked up to their table and kissed Cecily on the cheek.

"Not much. My friend here wants to meet you. You don't mind, do you?"

Javier looked over at Jennifer, who was stunned that he was standing at their table, actually talking to them.

"Javier, this is Jennifer." Cecily introduced them.

"Hi," he said to her, shaking her hand, and sitting down at the table with them.

"Um hi," was all Jennifer could get out of her mouth, still in shock.

Cecily and Javier both sat watching Jennifer for a moment, amused at her reaction, until Cecily broke the silence.

"So, come over to the bar later. I don't expect it to be busy, what with all the clean up work still going on. We can hang out," Cecily said to Javier.

"Yeah, sounds good. Well it was nice meeting you, Jennifer. See you later Cec, love you." With that, he walked away.

"Oh my god, I can't believe that just happened," Jennifer said to Cecily the second Javier was out of hearing range. She was completely starstruck. "And in all these years, how could you not tell me Javier Lopez was your best friend?"

"She speaks." Cecily was making fun of her, but her friend didn't seem to notice. "To me, he's just a guy that I grew up with. He's no different than any of my other friends. I don't tell you about all of them, do I?"

"Well, no. But, he's Javier Lopez. He's like the biggest celebrity ever. You should have told me about him. I'm mad at you now." Jennifer glared at Cecily and smiled. She was just kidding and Cecily knew it.

"You should come to the Wildflower tonight too. Hang out with Javier and me."

"I will." Jennifer would not have missed an opportunity to hang out with Javier Lopez for anything in the world.

"You know he's gay, right?"

"What?" Jennifer was clearly surprised by Cecily's announcement. "No he's not."

"Yeah, Sweetheart, he is. He doesn't announce it to the world because of his work and all. But, you are definitely not his type."

"Damn." Jennifer leaned back in her chair, disappointed.

"You can't tell anyone, okay?" It really wasn't a question. Cecily was serious.

"Okay, fine. I won't tell anyone. Can I still hang out with you guys?"

"Sure, why not."

Best friends since they were 8 years old, Cecily and Javier adored each other. They met one sunny summer day when Cecily walked into the local ice cream shop and sat down next to him. She lived only a block away and her mother let her walk to the shop alone. Javier was plump and shy and did his best to ignore her. Cecily didn't seem to notice though. She just chattered on for hours about everyone in town. It was in her nature from a young age to be gossipy and she just couldn't help it.

Javier couldn't help but like her. By the end of that summer, she had brought Javier out of his shell and they were inseparable. All these years later, Cecily still liked to take credit for Javier's fame. She often told people that if it weren't for her, he would still be the fat little shy boy they all remembered. Javier didn't mind that she took the credit. Heck, as far as he was concerned, she was probably right.

~

"Hey, Sweetheart. What's wrong?" Javier asked.

Javier was sitting at the bar waiting for Cecily to show up for her shift. He was between movies and had about a month off until filming started on the next one. He was going to play the lead in a new vampire series. He wouldn't win any big awards, that type of movie never did. But, he would make millions, and that was just fine with him. In the meantime, he hung out at the Wildflower bar a lot. It was a place that he knew was safe from his rabid fans. Cecily ran off anyone that bothered him. He loved passing the time with his best friend. When she walked in, she looked upset.

"Oh not much really," she said as she gave Javier a hug. "I'm just worried about the Carmichaels. Piper in particular."

"What's wrong with my girl, Piper? Should I go check on her?" Javier asked.

"No, it's just with Alex's death and Piper's involvement in that whole thing, you know, I'm just worried about her," Cecily told him.

"Yeah, me too. You know she has a crush on me, right?" He smiled at that.

"She's 15 years old and has a new crush every week. It's what 15 year olds do. Besides, everyone has a crush on you. Who can blame her?" Cecily was teasing Javier and he knew it.

"So true." Javier was teasing her back.

"Oh, there's Jennifer," Cecily announced, as her friend walked in.

Jennifer wasted no time sitting on the barstool right next to Javier. She didn't care that he was gay. He was a super famous celebrity and she wanted to get to know him. Her friends back home would be green with envy.

Javier and Cecily looked at each other and smiled. Jennifer's behavior was old news. They were used to it. Javier played along. He actually didn't mind much. It sometimes still surprised him that people were so drawn to him, especially after growing up so shy and quiet. He relished the attention now.

"Did you hear that Oscar Spencer is in town?" Cecily asked Javier.

"Yeah, I heard. It's all over town. Besides, I saw him at the memorial service," Javier answered.

"Who's that?" Jennifer asked.

Cecily and Javier proceeded to tell Jennifer all about Oscar, and about his son's murder. She was stunned and told them that she hadn't heard anything about it.

"You would think that would be on the news," she told them.

"Well it was here. But, there was an earthquake and wave that caused a lot of devastation and several people were killed. I guess Alex's death didn't really make national news," Cecily replied.

"That Oscar is a piece of work. He beat his wife and kids and then his wife killed herself. No one wants to mess with Oscar Spencer," Javier told her.

"Oh, Piper. Come here. I want you to meet someone," Cecily called to her as she walked through the bar.

Piper walked over and gave Javier a hug.

"Hey beautiful girl," he said to her. "How have you been?"

"Oh, fine, I guess. You know, a lot has been going on around here," she replied with a frown.

"Piper, this is my friend, Jennifer." Cecily introduced the two of them.

Jennifer and Piper greeted each other. The quartet spent the next hour talking about Alex, Oscar, Dixie, and everything else having to do with the case. There really was no need for Piper to hold back any further. Everyone on the island was already talking about the case. They all knew the story that Frankie and Dixie showed up first and found Alex fatally injured. Then Piper and Olivia showed up afterward. The problem was that other than that, no one knew anything for sure. Most of the island suspected either Frankie or Dixie, or both, were guilty. They arrived first. What other possible explanation was there? Piper wasn't so sure that it was either of them.

"Look," Piper told them, "I'm no fan of Frankie or Dixie, but honestly, I don't think either of them is capable of bashing in the head of someone like Alex."

"I heard he was pretty drunk," Javier said. "Was he?"

"That's what I heard too," Cecily added.

"Yeah, I know. But, who knows if that's the truth," Piper answered. "The gossip in this town is running rampant."

Piper looked sideways over at Cecily when she said that. Cecily just shrugged. She didn't even try to justify her actions. It was just who she was. Most of the town delighted in her stories. Cecily knew that and smiled at the thought.

CHAPTER 22

That night, Dixie laid in bed staring at the ceiling. It was after 1:00 a.m., but she couldn't sleep. She knew the whole town thought she was guilty and it scared her. The more she thought about it, the more she was convinced that Sawyer Hale was the guilty one. He had the most motive. Alex was harassing his girlfriend, Frankie. Sawyer had confronted him on the beach not long before she and Frankie found Alex lying there, unconscious. Yes, Sawyer was on the football team at school and was very handsome and popular, but that didn't mean he couldn't be guilty.

It wasn't fair, Dixie thought. Unfortunately, life was not always fair. Popularity and good looks could get away with a lot of things. She herself had counted on that fact most of her life. Regret started to creep in on her thoughts as she remembered her past behavior toward people that didn't have the fortunate genes that she was blessed with.

As she laid there thinking, she heard a creak on the stairs outside her room and it startled her back into the moment. She sat straight up in her bed, sure that someone was creeping up the stairs. She turned and watched her closed bedroom door, completely expecting it to open at any moment. Dixie pulled up the blankets in a protective manner and stared at the door for at least five full minutes. Nothing.

No more creaks, no shadows under her door, nothing at all. She was being silly and jumpy, she thought.

"Ugh, this is ridiculous. No one is here. I'm just being paranoid," she said to herself out loud, throwing off her blankets.

Though she knew she was just being jumpy, Dixie got up to peek out her bedroom door, just in case. There was a faint light shining in through the window, next to their front door. It made a sort of warm, cozy, yellow glow up the stairs and on the wall. She opened her door wide and walked to the bathroom, hearing no further noises. It's just an old house, she thought. It creaks all the time.

When she was done in the bathroom, she walked back quietly to her room, as she didn't want to wake her parents and little brother, who were all asleep down the hall from her room. Dixie pushed her bedroom door open and stood at the threshold looking in. She scanned the room one more time before she walked in, her heart racing. Finally realizing that her fear was unnecessary, she closed her door quietly and made her way to her bed in the nearly pitch black room.

That's when she saw him. Or it, rather. She saw a shadow. It very briefly crossed her room toward her bed. She took a deep breath and just as she was about to let out a blood curdling scream, a hand clamped over her mouth. What came out was a muffled, whiney sort of sound. Certainly nothing that could be heard more than a couple of feet from her bed.

Paralyzed with fear, Dixie became completely immobile. She had always thought of herself as a fighter and imagined that if she were ever attacked, she would fight to the death. But, reality overcame her when it actually happened. She couldn't move a muscle, no matter how hard her mind willed her limbs to move.

"Don't make a sound or I will kill your family," an eery voice whispered to her. She had no idea who it was. "My friend is down the hall watching your brother as we speak."

He was only inches from her, but she couldn't see his face. The room was too dark to see anything. She nodded her head, so he would know that she understood.

"I know you killed Alex Spencer and I'm going to make sure you fry for it. You better hope the sheriff arrests you. Because if he doesn't, I'm coming for you." His words became slower and evenly spaced. "You..got..that?"

Dixie nodded her head quickly, not daring to argue with him. She took his threats seriously and was terrified that his friend would hurt her family.

"We are leaving now. Don't you dare move or make a sound. If you do, your family is dead."

The intruder let Dixie go and walked out. When he opened the door, she could see a dark silhouette with the glow of the light from downstairs behind him. He was wearing black from head to toe, as far as she could tell, and had a black ski mask covering his face. He also had on black gloves. He turned to look at her one last time. She had not moved a muscle since he let her go. He closed the door behind him and walked down the stairs and left through the front door.

The second that Dixie heard the front door close, she jumped up and ran to her little brother's room and switched on the hall light. He was sleeping soundly. She walked in and put her palm on his back, just to make sure he was actually breathing. She didn't want to find any surprises in the morning. Then she went to her parents' room and opened the door. It was very dark, but she could hear her father snoring, so she knew they were okay.

"Mom, Dad, wake up," she called from the doorway. "I need to talk to you. It's important."

Her mother woke up first. "Dix? What's wrong?"

"I need to talk to you both. Someone just broke into the house and came into my room." That's when Dixie realized she was shaking from head to toe.

"Mitchell," her mother said, as she grabbed his arm and shook him.

"Mmm, what?" He had been sound asleep.

"Wake up. Someone broke into the house."

With that, he was wide awake and sat straight up in bed.

"Are they still here?" he asked.

"No, they left," Dixie replied.

"Dixie, are you okay?" he asked her as he got out of bed and walked to the doorway to hug his daughter.

"Y..yes, I'm okay."

"You're shaking, Sweetheart. Did he hurt you?"

"No." Dixie wrapped her arms tightly around her father's waist and started sobbing as her mother also got up to join them.

"What's going on in here?"

They all turned to see Dixie's little brother, MJ, standing in the hall rubbing the sleep out of his eyes.

"Everything's fine here," their mother told him. "Come on Buddy, I'll take you back to bed."

While her mother was putting MJ back in bed, Mitchell and Dixie walked downstairs and checked the locks on all the doors and windows. Just as they were finishing up, her mother, Dee, walked in. She made them hot chocolate and they all sat at the kitchen table.

"Okay, now tell us everything that happened," Mitchell ordered her.

Dixie spent the next few minutes detailing her terrifying experience. Even though the man said he had a friend with him, she wasn't so sure. She never heard or saw anyone else, and when he left, she only heard one set of footsteps on the stairs.

Mitchell Bradford called the sheriff, who showed up about an hour later and took a report. He told them that he would look into it. But, because the man was wearing gloves, they couldn't get fingerprints and it was unlikely that they would be able to catch him, unless he did it again. He advised that they install security cameras around the house.

By the time the sheriff left, it was after 3:00 a.m. and they all went back to bed. Dixie locked her bedroom door after making her father check under the bed and in the closet for her. She felt a bit foolish at 16 years old, having her father check her room for monsters, but it did make her feel better. Even after all that, she crawled under her covers and pulled them up to her chin and spent the rest of the night staring at her bedroom door. When the sun started to peek in through the slats in the blinds on her window, she had enough. She got up and wandered the house, double checking that all the doors and windows were still locked. They were.

Mitchell Bradford called that very day and ordered a security system and cameras for the house. With everything going on in town, and people believing that his daughter was a murderer, they didn't feel safe. They felt extremely lucky that the man, or men, that broke in did not harm Dixie. Mitchell shuddered just thinking about what might have been.

CHAPTER 23

The next day, Anna found Cecily sitting in the cafe eating breakfast and watching the ocean.

"Hi," Anna sat down at the table. She had grabbed a raisin muffin from the kitchen on her way out. "Wow, what a beautiful day. Not a single cloud in the sky." She set the computer down on the table in front of her.

"I'm sure you didn't come out here to talk about the weather," Cecily replied back. "What's up?"

"I thought you wanted my help. You don't need to be snarky with me." Anna tilted her head and raised her eyebrows Cecily's way.

"Sorry, Sweetheart. I'm just really tired this morning, and it's making me a bit cranky. Did you find something on the computer?"

"Well, yes and no," Anna told her. "I found out that the messages were coming from a computer at the hospital. But, there is no way to tell exactly who sent them. I can tell you that much. I had to hack into their servers to find that out. Someone logged into the open wifi network that the hospital gives out to anyone that wants to use it. Unfortunately, there is no way to tell who. It could be anybody."

"Damn. I was hoping for better news. Well, that's okay. I really appreciate your help anyway," Cecily told her.

"Who do you think sent the messages?" Anna asked her, curiously. "You have someone in mind, don't you?" She wasn't expecting Cecily to give up that information though.

"I honestly don't know at this point. Piper might have a better idea when I tell her it came from the hospital. She works there part time," Cecily replied.

"Yeah, maybe she does." Anna finished her raisin muffin.

"I just want to remind you that this is really personal and the fewer people that know, the better. Okay?" Cecily said to Anna as she stood up, picked up the computer and walked back into the inn. Anna didn't get the chance to answer her.

Cecily found Piper coming down the stairs from her room and explained to her everything that Anna had just told her.

"Oh wow. I have no idea who it could be at the hospital. I'll keep my ears open though when I'm at work. Maybe I can figure it out," Piper told her.

"Honey, just be careful. This person could be dangerous."

"I will," Piper replied.

Precisely at 6:00 a.m., eight days after little Zachary went missing, the Porters' bedroom phone woke them from a dead sleep.

"Hello." A groggy Marshall answered the phone.

"Marshall, Sheriff Rex here. We found your boy." Right to the point, as usual. Rex wasn't much for small talk.

Marshall was suddenly wide awake and reached over to shake his wife out of her slumber. "What? Are you sure?" he asked the sheriff.

"What is it?" Eliza asked him, crawling out of bed and picking up her pink robe from the floor. Her short blonde hair was sticking up everywhere.

"Just a second, Hun," he said to Eliza, as he held up his left index finger toward her and listened intently to the voice on the other end of the phone.

"Okay, sure, thank you," he said into the phone and hung up, turning to Eliza.

"Rex said they found Zach."

Eliza gasped. With her robe only half on, Eliza stopped what she was doing and turned to face Marshall. "What exactly did he say?"

"He just said Zach was found in another town and their social worker is on her way to Sea Cove with him. They will be boarding the ferry shortly. We are to meet them at the sheriff's office in an hour."

They both looked at each other, stunned into speechlessness.

One hour later, the Porters arrived at the Sheriff's Station. One look at their faces and Rex could see how anxious they were to get their son back. He thought of himself as an excellent judge of character.

"Sorry folks, they haven't arrived yet. Go over there and get some coffee." He pointed at the far corner of the tiny office kitchen. "Then come on into my office so we can talk while we wait."

Once the three of them sat down, the sheriff explained to them what happened.

"I talked to one of the deputies over in Big Oak and he said they got a call about midnight. There was this drifter that was at one of them all night diners. He had a small boy with him and the boy seemed upset. The whole thing seemed weird to the waitress, I guess. She had never seen a drifter with a small kid before and it concerned her. She tried to talk to the boy, but the drifter shut her down and the boy started crying for his mommy."

Rex looked over at Eliza then, who was digging for tissues in her purse. Marshall just sat in stunned silence.

"Anyway, the waitress just knew something wasn't right and she called the local sheriff. When they questioned the man, he said the boy belonged to a lady friend of his and he was just watching him. The man gave them the woman's name, but the sheriff couldn't find any trace of anyone with that name. No evidence of her at all, and the man couldn't give them her whereabouts. He told them he forgot where she lived. That's when they arrested him for kidnapping. And that's where we come in."

"Are they sure it's him?" Eliza looked hopeful to Rex.

"Well, they saw him on a poster. You know we have posters of your boy all over the state?" He waited for a response and they just nodded.

"The cops saw the poster and said it sure looks like him to them. We just need you to identify him when they arrive."

"Of course," Marshall replied.

"Well, that's the whole story, of what I know anyway," Rex added. "So, I'm going to leave you two for a few minutes. I need to make some phone calls. You can stay here in my office until they arrive, if you like."

Rex left and sat at one of the desks in the main office where the rest of the staff sat. He was the only one that had his own office. He was the sheriff after all. While he made his phone calls, he glanced over at Marshall and Eliza occasionally. It made his cranky heart feel good to give the two of them a happy ending to their story. He could see them talking in his office, but couldn't hear anything.

A few minutes later, the social worker walked in with the little boy and the Porters came out to greet them. The scared little boy reached for Eliza as she drew near. She took him and hugged him tight, her tears dribbling down the back of the boy's blue t-shirt.

"Well, it looks like my work is done here," Rex told them. "Take your son home. And please watch him more carefully." They both just nodded.

Rex smiled as they walked out the door, happy that the boy had been found and was unharmed.

The news spread all over the island with amazing speed. Marshall and Eliza had a couple of stops to make on their way home, one of them being the hardware store.

"Hey there, Porters," Dooley greeted them as the three of them walked in. "I heard you got little Zachary back. I'm so happy for you all."

"Thanks, Dooley. You heard already?" Marshall asked him.

"It's a small town, you know?"

Marshall knew. He had grown up on the island and knew all too well how secrets didn't last long at all there.

"Well, I never did come back to get the stuff I need for our rose garden. Remember I was here the day of the earthquake?"

"Oh yes, I remember," Dooley smiled. "I remember the both of us hitting the ground because we thought the building was going to fall down on our heads." He handed Zachary a grape lollipop as he was speaking. He kept a bowl full of them under his front counter to help keep the little ones entertained.

Zachary was still in his mother's arms and reached for it greedily as they all smiled.

"I put everything back when cleaning up, so you'll have to gather it all back up."

"Oh, of course. I didn't expect that you had it sitting here all this time," Marshall said.

"How's Dorothy doing? I haven't seen her in a while," Eliza asked as she pulled the sticky purple lollipop from her blouse. Zachary had carefully placed it there. She handed it back to him as he grinned mischievously.

"She's fine. Thanks for asking. She doesn't get out much, has a terrible case of rheumatoid arthritis. It keeps her home a lot."

"Oh, I'm sorry to hear that," Eliza replied. She made a mental note to stop by the house and visit. Dorothy had always been so nice to her.

The Porters wandered around the store for a few minutes, gathering the items they needed. After they paid for everything, they all said good-bye and were on their way.

Once they arrived home, several of their neighbors stopped by to congratulate them on getting Zachary back. The Porters were grateful for the nice words, but really just wanted to be left alone with their son. He had been gone eight days and they wanted him all to themselves.

CHAPTER 24

The next morning was Monday and Rex was sitting in the front area of the sheriff's office, where the deputies all had desks and they were all trading stories about their weekends. Rex was right smack in the middle of a not so riveting account of his round of golf on Saturday afternoon, when Oscar Spencer walked in.

"Are you kidding me, Rex? You are off golfing when you have my son's murder to solve?" Oscar was pissed off and belligerent.

Every person in the room stood, ready for the inevitable confrontation.

"Sheriff," Rex replied calmly. "You will address me as Sheriff."

"Whatever," Oscar shot back. "I'll call you whatever you want when I see that you are actually taking this seriously."

The two deputies in the room moved a bit closer to Oscar, but didn't engage him. Rex looked over at them. He knew that they knew what they were doing. He had trained them well and didn't have to give them any orders. Oscar saw them too. He stopped approaching the sheriff and stood his ground. He was no match for three officers that wanted nothing more than to take him down a peg.

"Mr. Spencer, why don't you come into my office, where we can talk?"

"No, I don't want to go into your office. I want some answers. Now. What exactly are you doing to find Alex's killer? Have you arrested Dixie Bradford yet?"

"I'm working on the case, like I told you before. It can take weeks or even months. You have to be patient," Rex told him.

"I don't have to do anything. You need to get off your fat ass and arrest that girl!"

Oscar started moving toward the sheriff again. The deputies stepped between Oscar and Rex.

"Sir, you need to step back," the taller of the two told him.

The deputy was a large man, who didn't put up with characters like Oscar Spencer. He gave Oscar a look that conveyed his seriousness, and Oscar backed up.

"I have a question for you," Rex said. "There was a break-in at the Bradford residence over the weekend. You have anything to do with that?"

Oscar hesitated just a moment longer than Rex was comfortable with. When someone needed time to think about their answer, it was always a lie.

"Um, no sir. I wouldn't know anything about that," Oscar finally replied.

"That's what I thought. We will talk about that more later."

"So what about you arresting the girl, Sheriff?"

Rex was rapidly losing his patience. "I think it's time that you leave my office."

"I'm not leaving until I get some answers." Oscar looked up at the deputy that was still standing in front of him with a scowl on his face, and stepped back a pace.

"Oscar," Rex began, "I'm going to say this in the nicest possible way I can think of, so that you will get my point. You need to back the fuck off and let me do my job. Got it?"

Rex was done dealing with Oscar. He turned around and walked back to his office and let the deputies deal with him. They could handle themselves just fine.

Oscar didn't even know how to respond to the sheriff. He stood, watching him walk away. Then he looked up at the deputies one more time and turned and walked out. He would have to figure out another way to deal with the lack of activity in the investigation.

Three hours later, Oscar and several buddies that he used to hang out at the bar and drink with all night, showed up in front of the Bradford house. They appeared to have started their nightly drinking ritual quite a bit earlier than usual. The group stood outside the house yelling and making obscene gestures. As they got louder and louder, more people showed up. Even neighbors that never had an issue with the Bradfords joined in.

Dixie called her father in a panic. She and her little brother, MJ, were the only two at home when it started. She tried to ignore them at first, figuring that was the best way to get them to just go away. But, it didn't work. As soon as they saw her peek out the window, it confirmed that she was home and things began to escalate. At that point, the crowd started getting out of control.

Once the mob mentality took over, chaos ensued and everything went into a downward spiral.

"Daddy, hurry!" Dixie told her father over the phone, just as something crashed through the front room window, causing Dixie to let out a shriek and drop the receiver.

"What the hell was that?" Mitchell asked his daughter. "Dixie?"

"Oh sorry, Dad. I dropped the phone. Someone threw a rock through the living room window. It almost hit MJ."

"Hang up the phone and both of you go upstairs and stay in your room with the door locked until I get there. I'm calling the sheriff," he ordered.

"Okay."

Dixie and MJ ran up the stairs and into her bedroom. She locked the door behind her, as ordered, and went to the window to watch the crowd in front of her house. There were at least 200 people running around on her street in full riot mode. They were throwing things at her house, jumping on cars parked on the street, and some were even carrying signs demanding that she be arrested. Dixie and her brother were terrified.

Dixie's eyes went wide when Javier Lopez jumped into the bed of a parked pickup truck and started yelling. Javier lived only two doors down from the Bradfords and was irritated over the crowd and noise. He couldn't be heard over the crowd and was getting nowhere. She watched him carefully as he got out of the bed of the truck and leaned into the open driver's window. Javier began honking the horn. It took almost a full minute to get their attention, but it worked. When the crowd stopped what they were doing to see what the honking was all about, he climbed back into the bed of the pickup and started yelling.

"Everyone needs to calm down right now!" he yelled to the crowd.

"She killed my boy!" Oscar Spencer yelled back.

By then, the street was silent, as the crowd stopped to listen to the exchange.

"You don't know that. Look everyone, I've known Dixie her whole life. I don't think she is capable of killing anyone," Javier replied, his voice much calmer.

"Everyone in town knows she did it. I want justice," Alex's father told him.

"Look, I know you want justice. Of course you do. We all do. But, this is not the way to go about it. If she is guilty, the sheriff will deal with her appropriately. Please, just let him do his job. This is getting you nowhere," Javier told the man.

As if right on cue, Sheriff Rex and his deputies pulled up and parked next to the truck Javier was standing in. Javier looked their way and relief flooded his face. He wasn't sure if he was going to be able to keep the situation calm much longer.

Rex got out of his car and noticed Javier standing in the back of the truck. He grabbed his bullhorn and joined Javier.

"Javier," Rex nodded. "Mind if I join you?"

"Hello Sheriff," Javier replied back. "Be my guest." Javier stepped aside to allow Rex more room.

"Sheriff!" Oscar yelled his way. "Have we got your attention now?"

"Oscar." Rex said into the bullhorn. The crowd was silent. "Have you lost your damn mind?"

Several of the rioters laughed at Rex's question. Oscar looked around him with a steely gaze and they went silent once again. Rex looked around and recognized almost every face in the crowd. He knew that they were good, decent people, who Oscar had riled up with his immediate need for someone to be held accountable for his son's death. Of course he wanted someone to be held accountable. Rex understood that. But, he also knew that rioting and terrorizing a poor teenage girl was not the way to go about it.

"We just want justice, that's all," Oscar replied, with much less enthusiasm as before.

Rex ignored his comment and addressed the crowd directly. "All of you need to go home. Except you Oscar," he said, pointing at the man. "If anyone is left standing here in five minutes, you will be arrested. Any questions?"

That was enough for the crowd to hear. They dispersed in short order. Not a single person stood in Oscar's defense. They were all worried about themselves. No one wanted to spend the night in jail for Oscar. He wasn't worth it.

As soon as the crowd was gone, Rex and Javier climbed out of the back of the truck. Rex thanked Javier for his help and told him to go back home.

"I don't have time to deal with this right now," Rex told Oscar. "All you succeeded in accomplishing was to take time out of my day and away from the investigation. I certainly hope you are happy."

"Arrest his ass," Rex told his deputies.

Rex enjoyed shaming Oscar. It didn't bother him a bit. Oscar was a thorn in his side, and he just wanted to be done with him. He glared at Oscar and stormed away. Just as Rex started heading to the Bradford's house to make sure the kids were all right, Mitchell Bradford pulled up.

The two of them went into the house as Dixie and MJ came down the stairs. Dixie told them everything that she had seen and experienced. They all seemed to have weathered the storm pretty well, considering, so Rex left. When he walked outside, the deputies and Oscar were gone.

When Rex arrived back at the sheriff's station, he let Oscar stew in his cell for a few hours. Eventually though, Rex knew that he would have to question him and formally charge him with something. He couldn't hold him long without doing those things.

"Why did you find it necessary to get into the middle of my investigation and harass that girl?" Rex asked Oscar during his formal questioning.

"I want to make sure she fries for what she did. You don't seem to be doing much of anything about it." Oscar was still upset and not backing down from the sheriff.

Rex sat there for a moment, thinking about what Oscar had just said.

"You want to make sure she 'fries' for it, huh? That's an interesting way of putting it. And, it is the exact term that the man who broke into the Bradford house used when he was holding poor Dixie hostage. You know, the man that terrorized a scared 16 year old girl."

Rex sat back to gauge his reaction. Oscar's face went pale. In that moment, Rex knew exactly what he needed to know. Oscar was the man that had broken into the house.

"Did you have an accomplice, or did you do it alone? I know you have lots of beer drinking buddies. One of them help you?" Rex asked him, matter-of-factly.

"I don't know what you are talking about," Oscar replied.

His words said one thing, his face said another. Rex was not fooled.

CHAPTER 25

"Who's up here?" Dixie asked as she rounded the top curve of the stairs in the lighthouse in the dark. She had gone there to think, just needing to be left alone for a little while. She had a flashlight with her, and aimed it at the noise on the top landing.

"Oh...you. Never mind. I'm leaving," she said when she saw who it was.

Hesitating for just a moment, and against her better judgment, Dixie went ahead and stepped onto the landing. Something was obviously wrong. She could see it in the landing occupant's eyes. "Are you okay?"

"I'm just here thinking, minding my own business."

Dixie watched as the person leaned over and picked something up off the floor of the landing.

"Are these your stupid bracelets?" Dixie was asked.

She recognized them as the bracelets she took off the other day when she and the girls were all in the lighthouse for their meeting. Dixie stood there in silence, watching them being flung, one by one, over the railing. She could hear them ping as each one hit the floor about 200 feet below them. She didn't say a word in protest.

"Why are you here, Dixie?" The words were a bit slurry.

"Are you drunk?" Dixie asked, noticing the empty bottle on the floor.

"Yeah. What do you care?"

"I don't," Dixie responded. "It's your life. Do whatever you want." She made sure to stay a safe distance away. "I'm leaving."

As Dixie turned to leave, the person at the top of the lighthouse started speaking. Dixie stopped and turned toward them.

"My life is over, you know. He's dead and I'll never see him again."

"Who? Alex? Is that who you're talking about?" Dixie asked.

"Yes, that's who I'm talking about. Who else?"

"Well, I didn't think you cared. Not really anyway." Dixie replied. "And you've been accusing me of killing him. So, why are you even talking to me now?"

"Someone has to be held responsible."

"Meaning what? Me? I'm the one that has to be held responsible?" Dixie asked.

"Yes, you. I can't just let this go. Someone has to pay. You know the sheriff isn't going to just let it go either."

"Maybe the real killer should be the one that has to pay," Dixie replied. "Maybe…oh." Dixie came to a disturbing realization.

The person standing before her smiled. "You figured it out. Didn't you?"

Dixie hesitated. "I, um, no. I don't know anything." Dixie turned to leave. "I need to go."

Even in an inebriated state, the killer jumped in front of Dixie, blocking the stairwell down.

"Why didn't you just give me the money?"

"What? You? You were the one blackmailing us? Why?" Dixie asked, completely surprised by the admission.

"I just wanted it so I could start a new life. And I certainly wanted to get off of this damn island for good. Your family can afford it. You should have just given it to me."

"I can't believe this is happening," Dixie replied, astonished. "After everything that has been happening, it was you this whole time?"

"I really wish you hadn't come here." The words were slurry, but the sentiment was undeniable.

"Look, I don't know anything and you're drunk. I'll keep my mouth shut. I don't really care who killed Alex." Dixie was starting to sound desperate.

"You won't keep quiet. You'll go running to the sheriff the second you walk out of this place. I can't let you do that."

Dixie decided at that moment that she had better do what she could to get out of the situation at hand. She was suddenly very afraid for herself. Dixie shoved the other person hard enough to knock them off balance, but they didn't fall. It was just enough for Dixie to start her descent of the lighthouse steps and hopefully get away.

Just as she rounded the second curve, she was suddenly taken off balance with a violent jerk of her head. The killer had grabbed a handful of her short hair and yanked her backward. Hard. Dixie didn't have time to react. Her feet went out from underneath her as she was pulled by her hair again, this time to the side. The winding staircase was very narrow, barely fitting a normal sized person. The second yank caused her to hurl over the side of the railing. Dixie began flailing her arms in a desperate attempt to grab onto something. Anything. But, it was too late. There was nothing for Dixie to grab onto to catch her fall.

After what couldn't have been more than two or three seconds, Dixie hit the concrete floor of the lighthouse with a sickening thud and the lighthouse went dark.

"Something's going on at the lighthouse," Cecily told Frankie when she found her working at the cafe the next morning.

Frankie stopped clearing the dishes and turned to Cecily. "What do you mean? What's going on?"

"I don't know yet. But, I'm going to find out. I just got a call from a friend that saw all the activity as she was driving to work this morning. She said there were so many cops there that someone must have died," Cecily explained.

"Frankie!" Piper yelled as she ran up the wooden steps to the cafe. She appeared to be in a panic.

Frankie and Cecily were both startled by Piper's sudden appearance and frantic manner.

"What? What's the matter?" Frankie asked, facing Piper and grabbing both of her upper arms in an effort to calm her down. "Take a deep breath and tell me what is wrong."

"It's Dixie. She's dead!" Piper burst out crying.

"What? No, that can't be true," Frankie replied. "Where did you hear that?"

"I was jogging on the beach this morning and I always run by the lighthouse. When I got there, the sheriff and coroner and a bunch of other people were there. The sheriff told me that they found Dixie dead. She fell from the landing at the top." Piper had run all the way to the cafe and was speaking so rapidly that she had to stop to catch her breath.

Frankie and Dixie were friends. Dixie was one of the few people in town that was nice to her when she arrived. Though Frankie and Piper weren't very close, Frankie hugged her and started crying.

Tears were starting to tumble gently out of her eyes and down Cecily's cheeks, as she watched the exchange between the two girls. She didn't even notice them as she struggled to find the words to comfort her friend Frankie.

"It was Oscar. It had to be," Frankie said, as she pulled back from Piper.

"No, he's in jail," Piper told her.

Cecily chimed in then. "No, he got out on bail yesterday."

CHAPTER 26

The small glass pane in the back door shattered and smashed to the kitchen floor in a louder commotion than what was expected. Olivia threw the rock back down into the backyard cacti garden. She stuck her hand through the window pane, careful not to cut herself, and twisted the deadbolt on the inside of the kitchen door, letting herself in. She had already peered into a couple of windows on her way into the backyard to make sure no one was home and found it deserted. Olivia was pleased with her sleuthing skills and how easily she was able to gain access to the sheriff's house.

She walked around the kitchen, opening cabinet after cabinet, not finding what she was looking for.

"Ah, here we go," Olivia said out loud when she opened the liquor cabinet in the living room. She reached in and pulled out a full bottle of vodka, twisted off the cap, and started drinking straight from the bottle. "Ugh, that shit's nasty," she said as she gagged. Then she took another long gulp. And another.

She wandered around the first floor of the house, taking the vodka along. When she found the sheriff's bedroom, it was too tempting not to snoop around. Overall it was pretty boring, nothing interesting at all, until she spied the shoebox on the top of the bedroom closet. When she pulled it down, she found a small gun in it.

"I can't believe that the sheriff is stupid enough to leave a gun where someone can find it. My lucky day."

She checked to see if it was loaded and it wasn't. It took her just a few minutes more to find the bullets hidden in the back of the closet and load the gun. Then she walked back into the living room with the vodka in one hand and the gun in the other. A deadly combination. She put the gun down on the coffee table temporarily to make a phone call.

"Hey Mary, this is Olivia," she said, once Mary answered. "Can you come over to Harley's house? I need to talk to you."

"Why are you at Harley's house? I thought they were on the mainland," Mary questioned.

"They are. I'm, um, house sitting. Can you come over?"

Mary looked out her bedroom window at the moon as it rose over the horizon where the dark sky met the restless sea. It was beginning to storm. "Yeah, I guess."

"Come in the back door, okay?"

"Okay. Be over there soon." Mary hung up.

Thunder exploded in the sky so loud that Olivia jumped. As she stood trying to catch her breath after the sudden jolt to her senses, she heard crunching footsteps on the broken glass in the kitchen behind her. She had just bent over to lay the phone on the table. She spun around to face Oscar Spencer.

"What the hell are you doing here?" she said to him. "How did you know I was here?" She started walking toward him in the kitchen and stopped, thinking better of it.

"I followed you," he smiled. It was a creepy, lechery sort of grin. It shot a shiver up Olivia's spine. "I waited outside for a while, until I was sure you were in here alone."

"You need to leave right now," she stated, pointing at the open kitchen door.

"No, I don't think so," he told her, closing the door behind him with his foot, without even turning around. His eyes never left Olivia's face.

"Why are you here?" she asked, backing away from him as he moved closer.

"What? I can't come see my daughter?"

"Ugh, no. I'm not your daughter. Never was, never will be. Get the hell out."

Olivia continued backing away from Oscar. When she backed into the coffee table, she realized that she had run out of room. The gun. Oh yes, she remembered the gun. As she turned to pick it up off the table, Oscar lunged at her. He jumped on her back, causing her to lose control of the gun and it went skidding across the floor. The fight was on.

Oscar started slamming her head into the floor as little white stars began floating around Olivia's vision. In a desperate attempt to free herself from the maniac, she reached up over her head, and behind her, and grabbed a big handful of his hair. She yanked as hard as she could, throwing him off balance. That was enough for her to elbow him hard in the face. He released her as he let out a howl of pain and grabbed his nose.

"You broke my nose, you stupid bitch!"

Oscar didn't even realize that Olivia had scurried across the floor and grabbed the gun. When he looked up, she was pointing it right at his head.

"What did you call me?"

"Um, nothing. What are you doing with that gun? You could hurt somebody."

"Yeah, that's kinda the point." Olivia was not backing down. After all the years of torment that he caused her, she finally had him where she wanted him.

"You're not gonna shoot me." Oscar said the words, but his voice was shaky with doubt.

"You sure about that? I really hate you and hated your son. You both should be dead."

"My son? Did you have something to do with Alex's death?" It had never occurred to Oscar that it was anyone but Dixie. "You and Dixie?"

"No, you idiot. Not me and Dixie. Just me. She had nothing to do with it." Olivia almost sounded boastful.

"What?" Oscar suddenly felt sick to his stomach.

"Yeah, I killed him," she told him as a smirk crawled across her face. "He's part of the reason my mother is dead. And you are the other part." She lowered the gun for just a moment, picked up the bottle of vodka and took a long drink. Her eyes never left Oscar.

"That bitch killed herself. I had nothing to do with that."

Olivia's body went rigid when Oscar spoke about her mother in that manner. She couldn't let him get away with that. Without even realizing what she was doing, she slowly set the bottle on the table next to her, lifted the gun she still held and pulled the trigger. Oscar dropped down to the ground. Hard.

"Oh my god, you shot him. What is going on?"

Olivia looked up to see Mary and Anna standing in the kitchen, both soaking wet.

"Just perfect," Olivia said. "Why did you bring her?" Olivia motioned toward Anna. "You shouldn't have brought her. Is it raining out?"

Mary didn't answer her questions. "Why did you shoot him?" she asked.

"He called my mother a bitch." In Olivia's intoxicated mind, that was a perfectly reasonable justification for shooting Oscar.

All three girls looked up as they heard the ceiling creak over their heads.

"Who's here?" Anna asked.

"That's a really good question. Why don't you go upstairs and find out?" Olivia told her.

Anna stood her ground. "No way."

"It wasn't a request. Go look!"

Olivia waved the gun in Anna's direction. Anna looked over at Mary, clearly afraid. They had just witnessed Olivia shoot Oscar, so they knew what she was capable of. Mary gave her a slight nod. Anna walked around Olivia and her gun, and headed up the stairs. Olivia and Mary stood in the kitchen in silence, listening. One minute later Anna descended the stairs, with Harley following.

"What are you doing here?" Olivia asked Harley. "I thought you were going to the mainland with your folks."

"I was," Harley replied, as she looked at the gun and back up to Olivia. "I wasn't feeling well, so I stayed home. I was taking a nap. Is that my dad's gun?"

"Don't worry about it." She looked at the three girls. "You all need to go sit on the couch." Olivia waved the gun at them and they obliged. "Put your phones on the table," she ordered.

Mary took her phone out of her shorts pocket and put it on the table. Anna told her that she didn't have her phone with her. Harley explained that her phone was upstairs, dead.

"I forgot to charge it," Harley said.

Olivia picked up Mary's phone and threw it against the kitchen wall. It landed in pieces on the kitchen floor, mixing in with the broken glass shards. None of the girls said a word.

"Mary, I saw some duct tape in one of the kitchen drawers. Go get it."

When Mary returned, Olivia told her to tape the girls' hands behind their backs. When Mary finished, Olivia put down the gun for a moment, out of reach, and taped Mary's hands.

"You killed Alex, didn't you?" Harley asked her.

CHAPTER 27

Olivia picked up the vodka and took a swig, wiping her mouth with her sleeve. She thought about her answer. What was the point in lying? She had broken into the sheriff's house, shot Oscar, and tied up three of her friends. What did she have to lose by telling the truth?

"So, what if I did?"

"This whole time it was you? After all of the meetings and accusations and stuff, you are the one that did it? I can't believe this." Mary was clearly upset. "You know that a lot of people think Frankie did it. And Dixie. How could you do that to them? We know that you hated Alex, but why did you have to kill him?" Mary asked.

Olivia looked around the room, and for the first time realized that they were all watching her intently. It made her incredibly self-conscious under all the scrutiny. She knew she was being judged, before she even had a chance to tell her side of the story.

"He was horrible to me. You know that," Olivia replied.

"I know. But just being bullied by someone is not enough of a reason to kill them," Anna chimed in.

"You don't know what you're talking about! Just shut up!" Olivia yelled at her.

"I'm sorry," Anna said, turning away from Olivia.

Olivia paced the floor as she tried to figure out what she was going to do. With Anna, Mary, and Harley knowing what she did, she was in danger. Danger of being arrested and spending the next 60 years in prison. She wouldn't do that. Couldn't do that. Prison was not an option for her.

"Olivia?" Mary spoke up.

"What?" she snapped, waving the gun wildly in the air, causing all three girls to duck instinctively.

"Why are you doing this? We didn't do anything to you and we won't tell anyone. I swear." Mary's voice was barely above a whisper.

Olivia ignored her. She took another drink of vodka, putting it down on the table, and peered out the window down the street. She half expected to see every law enforcement vehicle on the island parked in front of the house.

"Can we please just go?" Anna asked.

"Wanna know why I'm doing this?" Olivia completely ignored Anna's request.

None of the girls answered.

"He tormented me, okay? Alex was relentless. From the moment I got up in the morning, until the moment I went to bed at night, he beat on me, yelled at me, called me names, everything. It was horrible. And sometimes he even came in my room at night, dragged me out of bed, and slapped me around, just for the fun of it."

The girls sat quietly and listened to her story.

"I would show up at school with bruises, and once even a broken arm. No one noticed. No one cared. They were all terrified of Oscar and what he would do if they said anything. So no one did anything about it. I was only a kid, and no one did anything about it."

Olivia walked over and picked up the vodka bottle and took a long drink, barely noticing the burning in her throat. The gun never left her hand. The three girls didn't move a muscle.

"It's his fault my mother is dead. You know that, right?"

The girls nodded.

"Him and his dad. Both of them are the reason she took the pills and killed herself. I hated them and wanted them both dead. Oscar left us right after she died. I couldn't get to him, but I could get to Alex." She was starting to sound quite drunk to the girls.

"That asshole had it coming. I got him to meet me at the Cove by telling him Frankie asked me to get him there. He was all for it. Idiot. I gave him a six pack and told him to go wait. I knew he would drink all of it and would be wasted by the time I got there. And I was right. He could barely stand up. So stupid."

"Maybe you should put the gun down. We can just sit here and talk," Harley tried coaxing.

"Shut up! I'm not putting it down. Do you want to hear the rest of the story or not?"

Harley nodded, terrified of opening her mouth.

"When I got to the Cove, he was sitting in the sand and barely recognized me. All of the beer was gone. We got into a huge fight about his father, and about Frankie. When he threatened to beat me, I had enough. He had stood up when we were fighting, but then stumbled over his own two feet and fell down. That was my chance. I picked up the nearest rock that I could lift and bashed him as hard as I could in the head. His head was partially caved in and he was knocked out instantly."

Olivia paused for only a moment, recalling that day.

"I thought he was dead, but then he started mumbling and lifted his right hand up to feel his head. So, I hit him again. And again. That was it. At least I thought it was. I threw the rock down and ran back to the beach party. Everyone was so involved in drinking and making out that no one even noticed me."

Olivia burst out crying after her confession. Anna, Mary, and Harley looked at each other. They just sat still on the couch and let her cry. After a few minutes, her sobs subsided and she was able to continue.

"I was afraid I would go to prison," she said, wiping the snot and tears from her face with her shirt sleeve. "I knew no one would believe it was just an accident."

"Why didn't you tell us? Maybe we could have helped you," Mary asked her.

"Yeah right. Like you would have helped me cover it all up."

"I don't know. But, you should have told us anyway," Mary said.

"Didn't I tell you to shut up?"

Mary nodded.

"Then Piper said she was going over to the Cove to find Frankie and it all just worked out perfectly from there. We found Frankie and Dixie standing over Alex, which made them look really guilty. No one even considered that it was me. Then the earthquake and wave. I couldn't have asked for a better scenario. All the stars lined up for me that day," Olivia smiled.

Olivia briefly sat down on a chair across from the couch that the three girls were sitting on.

"You all know that Frankie and Alex were seeing each other, don't you?"

Mary raised her eyebrows. She had been completely unaware of Frankie and Alex's relationship.

Before anyone could answer, Olivia slammed her empty palm against her mouth. "Oh god," she said as she jumped up and sprinted for the bathroom, still holding the gun in her other hand.

"Do you think that's true?" Mary asked Anna.

"Frankie and Alex?" Anna asked. "I thought she hated him. Wasn't he stalking her?"

Mary just shrugged her shoulders. "I don't know. No one tells me anything."

"She's gone now. Can you get out?" Harley asked. "My arms are killing me."

"No, it's too tight. Do you think she's gonna kill us?" Mary asked, her eyes watering up. She was trying her best to be brave. But, when faced with a drunk killer, wielding a loaded gun, teenage girl or not, it was scary. Mary was terrified. All of the girls were.

"I don't know," Anna replied. "She's just crazy enough to do anything. We need to get her to stop drinking. Maybe we can reason with her if she's sober. We definitely can't when she's drunk."

"I have an idea," Mary said. "I think I can reach the bottle with my foot." Mary kicked out her leg and the bottle went spinning across the floor and slid right under the chair across from them. The same one Olivia had been sitting in. "Maybe she won't notice it's gone."

A few minutes later Olivia emerged from the bathroom, looking a bit more sober. She had washed her face and cleaned herself up after she hurled up most of the vodka she had consumed.

"Okay, where was I? Oh yeah, Frankie and Alex," Olivia continued as she sat down on the chair, still holding the gun. "Three days before the wave, I was at the cafe with my foster mom, getting smoothies. When I went to go to the bathroom, I heard Frankie and Alex arguing in the hallway. They kept their voices low, so no one would hear them, but I stood there listening anyway." Olivia looked over at the girls. "You three paying attention?"

"Yes," they answered in unison.

All the girls had to make a concerted effort to not shift their eyes to the floor below Olivia. They didn't want to remind her that there was still more alcohol to consume. She seemed to have completely forgotten about it as she continued her story.

Everyone turned toward the front door when there was a knock on it.

CHAPTER 28

"Who the hell is that?" Olivia asked, as she walked to the living room window and looked out. "Oh great."

Olivia walked over and opened the door and stepped aside to allow Frankie and Piper to walk into the house. They took one look at the three girls sitting on the couch, tied up, and turned back to face Olivia. As they did, they came face to face with the gun she was holding.

"Go sit on that other couch," Olivia told them, using the gun to motion toward the couch.

She had Piper tape up Frankie's wrists, then Olivia taped up Piper's. She stood back and took in the scenery.

"Who is that lying on the floor?" Frankie asked when she noticed the body and all the blood.

Olivia glanced in his direction. "Oh, that's just Oscar. He was pissing me off."

The girls all looked at each other, but none said a word. They could see, first hand, that Olivia was capable of killing someone.

"What are you two doing here anyway?" Olivia asked.

"My mom sent us looking for Mary and Anna. Mary told me that they were coming here," Piper told her.

"So no one else knows? Your parents?" Olivia asked Piper.

"No, they don't know." Piper immediately wished that she had lied. If Olivia thought others knew they were there, she might let them go, for fear of being caught.

"Well, now it's a party. Where's the vodka?" Olivia asked, looking around the room.

She watched as Mary and Anna's eyes shot straight to the spot under the chair where Mary had kicked the bottle. Olivia bent down and retrieved it. She took a long drink out of the bottle, which was only about half full. The girls could see that Olivia was getting quite drunk.

"So, let's continue our story, shall we?" Olivia turned to Frankie. "I was just telling them all about you."

Frankie's eyebrows raised. "What about me?"

"I was talking about your argument with Alex at the cafe. I heard everything. Here's the rest of the story. Apparently it was just a one or two time thing, her and Alex. It didn't sound like they had been dating or anything. They were fighting about Sawyer." Olivia glared at Frankie. "Alex was pissed off that she was still seeing Sawyer, and Frankie sounded like she was trying to get rid of Alex. Alex was threatening to tell Sawyer and they were arguing viciously about it."

"That's a lie!" Frankie yelled.

"Shut up! I'm the one talking here."

Olivia got up and walked to the kitchen. She hunted in the cupboards and found a glass and poured herself some ice water from the refrigerator. She walked back and sat down, just as another round of thunder roared overhead and they all looked up instinctively. Lightning flashed and they could hear it pouring rain, but the curtains were drawn, so they couldn't see any of it.

"Don't you find what I said interesting? I mean, I could make sure that everyone knew that Frankie was sleeping with Alex. That would make her look really guilty. Don't you think?"

Olivia looked back and forth at each girl. None said a word.

"Well? Answer me!" Olivia yelled, as she pointed her gun at the girls.

"Yes, it would make her look really guilty," Anna answered rapidly.

"And I heard that's why Sawyer dumped her. Hilarious," Olivia added.

Mary started to cry.

"Seriously? What are you crying about?" Olivia was not in the mood to deal with a crier.

"I'm sorry. I can't help it," Mary answered. "Frankie is my friend. You are the one that killed Alex, not her."

"Stop it right now or I will shoot you. I mean it… wait. Better yet, I'll shoot Anna. How would you like that? I can't shoot Frankie. She still might be the one that goes away for this." Olivia pointed the gun at Anna.

"Okay, I'm stopping." Mary's crying stopped immediately. She was terrified that Anna would be shot and she couldn't be responsible for that.

"You killed Dixie too, didn't you?" Frankie asked her, terrified of the answer Olivia would give.

"She didn't give me much choice," Olivia replied and took another drink of vodka. "Anyone want some?" She held out the bottle in front of her as they all shook their heads. "Whatever. More for me."

"Why did you have to kill Dixie? She didn't do anything to you." Frankie was trying her best not to cry at the revelation from Olivia.

Olivia thought about her answer for a few seconds. "Well, two reasons actually. One, she figured it out. I couldn't let her go to the cops, could I? No, that would be stupid. And two, she wouldn't give me the money I wanted. If she had just gotten the $10,000 for me, I would have been able to leave this god forsaken island and never look back."

"You are the one that was blackmailing us?" Piper asked, her mouth hanging open.

"Don't look so surprised. Who did you think it was? You all are the dumbest people I have ever met." Olivia started pacing the room, stumbling a bit. She was clearly intoxicated.

Mary spoke up before Olivia started talking again. "What about the video you talked about in the messages? Was someone else there with you?"

Olivia rolled her eyes heavenward. "There is no damn video. Seriously, you can't be that stupid. I just said that to get money out of you all."

Mary looked down, without responding.

"What are you going to do now?" Harley asked. "We can't just sit here forever."

"A lot can happen between now and forever," Olivia told her.

Harley just lowered her eyes to the coffee table in front of her. She was reminded of the time when she was 4 years old and tripped over their chihuahua and landed face first on the edge of that same coffee table. She still had the scar on her forehead to prove it.

Olivia stopped her pacing and turned to face Harley. "You know, that's a good point. You all know my secrets now. I should just shoot all of you and get it over with." She pointed the gun at each girl individually, causing each of them to cringe when the gun was in their face.

"Who wants to go first?" Olivia smiled when she said that. She was not expecting a response. "You know, I didn't want to kill anyone else. Well, no one at all actually. But, Alex deserved it. He was a despicable human being. I'm not even sorry about that one. Then Dixie figured it out and I had no choice. Then Oscar here." Olivia tilted her head briefly in his direction without looking his way. "He showed up and attacked me. That one was self defense. Now you all are here. If I let you go, you'll go straight for the sheriff. I won't spend my life in prison."

"No, Olivia, you don't need to do this. We want to help you," Piper told her. "We're your friends. Let us help."

"Friends? Yeah, I don't think so. Not a single one of you paid five minutes of attention to me before the day of the beach party. Then you only did so because I happened to show up and see Frankie and Dixie standing over Alex's body. You know the whole 'keep your frenemies closer' thing, right? Frenemies, that's a funny word. Wait, that's not how it goes." Olivia started laughing.

Piper interrupted Olivia's amusement at her own words. "Olivia, listen, we are your friends. I mean it. We have all gotten close over these past few weeks and we don't want to see you go to jail. Look, if you just let us all go, we will round up enough money for you to leave. We will never say anything to anyone."

Olivia watched Piper carefully while she was speaking. She wanted to see if she could figure out if Piper was telling the truth or not. She wanted desperately to believe Piper. But, drunk or not, Olivia was not stupid enough to think that none of the girls would tell anyone. Especially the sheriff's daughter, who was sitting in front of her, tied up with the rest.

"How would you get the money?" Olivia asked. She was very cautious.

The girls all looked around at each other.

"Yeah, that's what I thought. None of you have a clue how to come up with $10,000," Olivia told them, as she walked toward them again. She was no longer holding the vodka bottle. Only the gun was in her hand.

"Like I said, which one of you wants to go first?" The room went dead silent as she heard five ticks from the clock on the wall. "What, no volunteers? Fine. Have it your way. You," Olivia said, pointing her gun straight between Harley's eyes. "I never liked you much. You get to be first."

Harley shrunk back into the couch as far as she could, squeezed her eyes tight, and waited for the inevitable. She prayed that there would be no pain. Just as Olivia was about to pull the trigger, all four sets of eyes, except Harley's, as hers were still squeezed shut, focused on something behind Olivia. This did not go unnoticed by Olivia. She turned around to see what had caught their attention.

"What are you all looking…"

She didn't get the chance to finish her sentence as Oscar jumped on her. Because Olivia's hand was still on the trigger, the gun went off and the bullet lodged in the wall over Harley's head. Harley shrieked. The gun was knocked out of Olivia's hand and it skidded across the floor, finally resting under the couch that Frankie and Piper were sitting on. No one even noticed where it went. They were all watching the fight. After Oscar surprised Olivia, they fought violently, completely forgetting about everyone else in the room. Even with Olivia's small stature, she wasn't going down easy. She gave it her all.

Just as another round of thunder hit, there was a deafening thud, so loud it could be heard over the thunder. They all looked to see Oscar standing there, bloody and beaten, over Olivia. Olivia was unconscious from being thrown, head first, into the bricks around the fireplace. No one knew if she was alive or not, and didn't want to know.

Oscar untied the girls and all five of them ran out the front door of the house, just as the police cars, sirens blazing, pulled up to the house. Someone had heard the gunshot and called them. Every officer from the three squad cars jumped out and protected themselves by standing behind their cars.

The sheriff was with them. He had been trying to call Harley for hours. Without a response from her, he got worried and headed back to the island, just in time.

One of the deputies rushed to the girls and herded them away from the house. Just as they reached safety, the front door opened. Every police officer pulled out their gun and aimed it for the front door.

Oscar walked out with the gun in his hand by his side. He was a bruised, bloody mess, and was barely recognizable. Olivia had returned Oscar's beating with an equally aggressive one.

"Sir, put down your weapon!" one of the deputies yelled at him.

Oscar hadn't even realized that he was holding the gun. He saw it sticking out from under the couch and instinctively picked it up so that Olivia wouldn't get it, if she woke up.

Then the unthinkable happened. Oscar lifted the gun and aimed it at the police. He knew they would blame him for Dixie's and Olivia's deaths. He wasn't going down without a fight. That's all it took. Oscar went down in a hailstorm of bullets as Mary screamed. Frankie knew how sensitive Mary was and did her best to block Mary from the view of the carnage. Unfortunately they could still hear everything, and knew exactly what was going on only a few feet from where they crouched behind one of the squad cars. None of the other girls said a word.

As soon as the gunfire stopped, Mary quieted down. Immediately, there was an eerie, unnerving quiet, after the cacophony of just a few seconds earlier. That's when they all heard an unexpected noise off in the distance. Another type of wailing sound, different from the one Mary had just been making. Every single person outside suddenly realized where it was coming from and turned to look at the house.

"It's Olivia. She's alive!" Piper yelled.

"Does she have a gun or other weapon?" Rex asked her.

"No, I don't think so. The gun Oscar had was all we saw her with," Piper told him, not daring to look at Oscar's body lying on the front porch of the sheriff's house.

The sheriff headed for the front door. He was inside no more than ten seconds when he yelled for the paramedics. They were already on site and ran inside. Everyone emerged a few minutes later, with Olivia handcuffed to the gurney she was on. They loaded her onto the waiting ambulance and drove away.

The deputies cordoned off the area around Oscar's body and the house.

Harley flew into her parents' waiting arms and they all cried. Once they calmed down a bit, the girls told the sheriff exactly what happened. Every excruciating detail. They all knew that Oscar had saved their lives and he was redeemed from his past mistakes in their eyes.

Over the next few weeks, Olivia recovered nicely in the hospital. Once released, she was charged with the deaths of Alex Spencer and Dixie Bradford. Olivia was convicted and sentenced to 20 years in prison. Because she was a minor, they decided against the death penalty.

It took a lot of time, and some professional help, but Piper, Mary, Frankie, Anna, and even Harley recovered from their ordeal.

Over time, Wildflower Island also recovered. Since the killer had been apprehended, and the kidnapper of Zachary Porter had also been arrested, the residents felt like they could sleep better at night.

But after everything…most began locking their doors at night.

Get the next book in the series.
DESPERATION ON WILDFLOWER ISLAND

When people start dying in unusual ways on Wildflower Island, the residents are in a panic. Is there a serial killer on the island? Are these just unfortunate accidents? As the answers begin to surface, secrets, deep and twisted, are discovered. Secrets that no one wants revealed.

The complete Wildflower Mystery Series:
Secrets of Wildflower Island
Desperation on Wildflower Island
Storm on Wildflower Island
Thorns on Wildflower Island

If you enjoyed this book and would like information on new releases, sign up for my newsletter here:

www.MichelleFiles.com
Thank you!

Printed in Great Britain
by Amazon